CHAPTER ONE

JANUARY had arrived with an absolute vengeance. Standing in the window behind her father's desk, Mia watched the way the wind was hurling the rain against the glass in fiercely gusting squalls—while behind her a different kind of storm was raging, one where two very powerful men pitched angry insults at each other.

Not that she was taking much notice of what they were actually fighting about. She knew it all already, so her presence here was really quite incidental.

Merely a silent prop to use as leverage.

'Look, that's the deal, Doumas!' she heard her father state with a brittle grasp on what was left of his patience. 'I'm not into haggling so either take what's on offer or damn well leave it!'

'But what you are proposing is positively barbaric!' the other man hit back furiously. 'I am a businessman, not a trader in white slavery! If you have difficulty finding a husband for your daughter try a marriage agency,' he scathingly suggested, 'for I am not for sale!'

No? Way beyond the point of being insulted by remarks like that one, Mia's startlingly feminine mouth twitched in a cross between bitter appreciation for the clever answer Alexander Doumas had tossed back at her father and a grimace of scorn. Did he truly believe he would be standing here at all if Jack Frazier thought he couldn't be bought?

Jack Frazier dealt only in absolute certainties. He was a rough, tough, self-made man who, having spent most of his life clawing his way up from nothing to become the corporate giant he was today, had learned very early on that attention to fine detail before he went in for the kill was the key to success.

He left nothing whatsoever to chance.

Alexander Doumas, on the other hand, was the complete antithesis of Jack. He was smooth, sleek and beautifully polished by a top-drawer Greek pedigree which could be traced back so far into history it made the average mind boggle, only, while the Frazier fortunes had been rising like some brand new star in the galaxy during the last thirty odd years, the Doumas fortunes had been steadily sinking—until this man had come on the scene.

To be fair, Alexander Doumas had not only stopped the rot in his great family's financial affairs but had spent the last ten years of his life repairing that rot, and so successfully that he had almost completely reversed the deterioration—except for one final goal.

And he was having the rank misfortune of coming up against Jack Frazier in his efforts to achieve that one goal.

Poor devil, Mia thought with a grim kind of sympathy, because, ruthless and unswerving though he was in his own way, Alexander Doumas didn't stand a chance of getting what he wanted from her father, without paying the price Jack Frazier was demanding for it.

'Is that your final answer?' Jack Frazier grimly challenged, as if to confirm his daughter's prediction. 'If so, then you can get out for I have nothing left to say to you.'

'But I am willing to pay double the market price here!'

'The door, Mr Doumas, is over there...'

Mia's spine began to tingle, the fine muscles lining its long, slender length tensing as she waited to discover what Alexander Doumas was going to do next.

He had a straight choice, the way she saw it. He could walk out of here with his arrogant head held high and his monumental pride still firmly intact, but put aside for ever the one special dream that had brought him to this point in the first place, or he could relinquish his pride, let his own

"Are we going to marry?"

"Yes, we will marry. We will do everything expected of us to meet your father's filthy terms! But don't," he warned, "let yourself think for a moment that it is going to be a pleasure."

"You seem to think you have the divine right to stand there and be superior to me. But you do not," she muttered. "You have your price, just like the rest of us! Which makes you no better than my father—no better than myself!"

"And what exactly is your price?" he challenged grimly. "Give me one good reason why you are agreeing to all of this and I might at least try to respect you for it!"

MICHELLE REID grew up on the southern edges of Manchester, England, the youngest in a family of five lively children. But now she lives in the beautiful county of Cheshire with her busy executive husband and has two grown-up daughters. She loves reading, the ballet, and playing tennis when she gets the chance. She hates cooking and cleaning, and despises ironing! Sleep she can do without, and she produces some of her best written work during the early hours of the morning.

Books by Michelle Reid

HARLEQUIN PRESENTS®
1859—THE MORNING AFTER
1917—GOLD RING OF BETRAYAL
2014—THE MARRIAGE SURRENDER

Don't miss any of our special offers. Write to us at the following address for information on our newest releases.

Harlequin Reader Service
U.S.: 3010 Walden Ave., P.O. Box 1325, Buffalo, NY 14269
Canadian: P.O. Box 609, Fort Erie, Ont. L2A 5X3

MICHELLE REID

The Price of a Bride

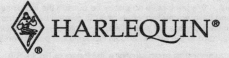

TORONTO • NEW YORK • LONDON
AMSTERDAM • PARIS • SYDNEY • HAMBURG
STOCKHOLM • ATHENS • TOKYO • MILAN • MADRID
PRAGUE • WARSAW • BUDAPEST • AUCKLAND

ISBN 0-373-12033-8

THE PRICE OF A BRIDE

First North American Publication 1999.

Copyright © 1998 by Michelle Reid.

principles sink to Jack Frazier's appalling level and pay the price being asked for that dream.

'There has to be some other way we can resolve this,' he muttered.

No there isn't, Mia countered silently. For the simple reason that her father did not *need* another way. The Greek had called Jack Frazier barbaric, but barbarism only half covered what her father really was. As she, of all people, should know.

Jack Frazier didn't even bother to answer. He just sat there behind his desk and waited for the other man to give in to him or leave as suggested.

'Damn you to hell for bringing me down to this,' Alexander Doumas grated roughly. It was the driven sound of a grudging surrender.

The next sound Mia heard was the creak of old leather as her father came to his feet. It was a familiar sound, one she had grown to recognise with dread when she was younger, and even now, at the reasonably mature age of twenty-five, she was still able to experience the same stomach-clutching response as she had in childhood.

Jack Frazier was a brute and a bully. He always had been and always would be. Man or woman. Friend or foe. Adult or child. His need to dominate made no exceptions.

'Then I'll leave you to discuss the finer details with my daughter,' he concluded. 'Get in touch with my lawyer tomorrow. He will iron out any questions you may have, then get a contract drawn up.'

With that, and sounding insultingly perfunctory now that he had the answer he wanted from the other man, Jack Frazier, cold, cruel, ruthless man that he was, walked out of the room and left them to it.

And with the closing of the study door came quite a different silence. Bitter was the only word Mia could come up with to describe it—a silence so bitter it was attacking the back of her neck like acid.

I should have left my hair down, she mused in the same dry, mockingly fatalistic way she had dealt with all of this.

It was the only way, really. She couldn't fight it so she mocked it. It was either that or weep, and she'd done enough weeping during her twenty-five years to know very well that tears did nothing but make you feel worse.

'Drink?'

The sound of glass chinking against fine crystal had her turning to face the room for the first time since the interview had begun. Alexander Doumas was helping himself to some of her father's best whisky.

'No, thank you,' she said, and stayed where she was, with her arms lightly folded beneath the gentle thrust of her breasts, while she watched him toss back a rather large measure.

Poor devil, she thought again. Men of his ilk just weren't used to surrendering anything to anyone—never mind to a nasty piece of work like her father.

Alexander Doumas had arrived here this afternoon, looking supremely confident in his ability to strike a fair agreement with Jack Frazier. Now he was having to deal with the very unpalatable fact that he had been well and truly scuppered—caught hook, line and sinker by a man who always knew exactly what bait to use to catch his prey. And even the fine flavour of her father's best malt whisky wasn't masking the nasty taste that capture had placed in his mouth.

He glanced at her, his deep-set, dark brown Mediterranean eyes flicking her a whiplashing look of contempt from beneath the glowering dip of his frowning black eyebrows. 'You had a lot to say for yourself,' he commented in a clipped voice.

Mia gave an empty little shrug. 'Better men than me have taken him on and failed,' she countered.

She was referring to him, of course, and the way he grimaced into his glass acknowledged the point.

'So you are quite happy to agree to all of this, I must presume.'

Happy? Mia picked up the word and tasted it for a few moments, before deciding ruefully, that—yes—she was, she supposed, *happy* to do whatever it would take to fulfil her side of this filthy bargain.

'Let me explain something to you,' she offered in a tone gauged to soothe not aggravate. 'My father never puts any plan into action unless he is absolutely sure that all participants are going to agree to whatever it is he wants from them. It's the way he works. The way he has *always* worked,' she tagged on pointedly. 'So, if you are hoping to find your redemption through me, I'm sorry to disappoint you.'

'In other words—' His burning gaze was back on her again '—you are willing to sleep with anyone if Daddy commands it.'

'Yes.' Despite the deliberate insult, her coolly composed face showed absolutely nothing—no hint of offence, no distaste, not even anger.

His did, though, showing all of those things plus a few others all meant to label her nothing better than a trollop.

Maybe she was nothing better than a trollop, allowing her father to do this to her, Mia conceded. Certainly, past history had marked her as a trollop.

'Did you do the choosing yourself?' he asked suddenly. 'Is that what this is really all about?'

Taken by surprise by the suggestion, her eyes widened. Then she laughed—a surprisingly pleasant sound amidst all the bitterness and tension. 'Oh, no,' she said. 'You said yourself that my father is a barbarian. It would go totally against his character to allow me to choose anything for myself. But how conceited of you to suggest it...' she added softly.

'It had to be asked,' he said, stiffening slightly at the gentle censure.

'Did it?' Mia was not so sure about that. 'It seems to me that you're seeing yourself as the only victim here, Mr Doumas,' she said more soberly. 'And at this juncture it may well help if I remind you that there tend to be different kinds of victims in most disasters.'

'And you are a victim of your own father's tyranny—is that what you are trying to tell me?'

His scepticism was clear. Her green eyes darkened. If Alexander Doumas came to know her better he would take careful note of that. She was Jack Frazier's daughter after all.

'I am not *trying* to tell you anything,' Mia coolly countered. 'I don't have to justify myself to you, you see.'

After all, she thought, why should she defend herself when his own reasons for agreeing to this were not that defensible?

Not that he was seeing it like that, she wryly acknowledged. Alexander Doumas was looking for a scapegoat on which to blame his own shortcomings.

'No,' he murmured cynically. 'You merely have to go to bed with me.'

And she, Mia noted, was going to be his scapegoat.

'Of course, I do understand that my lot is the much easier one,' she conceded, with that same dangerously deceptive mildness. 'Being a woman, all I need to do is lie down, close my eyes and mentally switch off, whereas you have to bring yourself to…er…perform. But God help us both,' she added drily, 'if you find me so repulsive that you can't manage it because we will really have a problem then.'

She had managed to actually shock him, Mia was gratified to note—had managed to make him look *at* her and *see* her, instead of just concentrating on showing her his contempt.

With a wry smile of satisfaction she deserted her post by the window at last to come around her father's desk and walk across the room towards the two high wing-backed leather armchairs that flanked the polished mahogany fireplace.

A log fire was burning in the grate, the leaping flames trying their best to add some warmth to a room that did not know the meaning of the word—not in Jack Frazier's house, anyway.

But the flames did manage to highlight the rich, burnished copper of Mia's hair as she walked towards them. Although she didn't look at Alexander Doumas as she moved, she felt his narrowed gaze following her.

Eyeing up the merchandise, she thought, cynically mocking that scrutiny.

Well, let him, she thought defiantly as she felt his gaze sweep over the smooth lines of her face, which she had been told was beautiful although she did not see any beauty in it herself.

But, then, she didn't like herself very much and they did say that beauty was in the eyes of the beholder.

Therefore, it followed that neither would this man be seeing any beauty in her right now, she supposed, as he was so actively despising her at this moment.

Oh, she was no hound-dog. Mia wasn't so eaten up with self-hate that she couldn't see that her hair, face, body and legs combined to present a reasonably attractive picture.

Whatever this man was feeling about her right now, she knew that he had looked at her before today and had wanted her so his expression of distaste simply failed to impress her.

Reaching the two chairs, she turned, felt his gaze dip over the slender curves of her figure—so carefully muted by the simple coffee-coloured pure wool dress she was wearing—and chose the chair which would place him directly in her sight so she could watch those eyes draw down the long length of her silk-stockinged legs as she sat and smoothly crossed one knee over the other.

Alexander Doumas was no hound-dog himself, Mia had

to acknowledge. In fact, she supposed he was what most fanciful females would have seen as ideal husband material—tall, tanned and undeniably handsome, with the kind of tightly contoured Greek-god body on which top designers liked to hang their very exclusive clothes.

Indeed, that iron grey silk suit looked very definitely top designer wear. He wore his straight black hair short at the back and neat at the front, and the rich smoothness of his olive-toned skin covered superb bone structure that perhaps said more about his high-born lineage than anything else about him.

He had a good mouth, too—even if it was being spoiled by anger and disgust at the moment—and his long, rather thin nose balanced well with the rest of his cleanly chiselled features.

But it was his eyes that made him special—deep-set, dark brown, lushly fringed, deceptively languid eyes that, even when they were showing disdain, could still stir the senses.

Her senses, she noted as she watched those eyes settle on the point where her slender legs disappeared under the hem of her dress and felt a warm, tingling sensation skitter along her inner thighs in response.

'Well,' she prompted, unable to resist the dig, 'do you have a problem there?'

He stiffened, the finely corded muscles along his strong jawbone clenching when he realised he had been caught staring. 'No,' he admitted on a rasping mutter.

At least he's being honest about it, Mia reflected ruefully. And so he should be, having spent the last month trying to get her into his bed!

'Then your only problem,' she went on coolly, 'is having to decide whether you want your lost island of Atlanta— or whatever it is called,' she mocked flippantly, 'badly enough to relinquish your single status to get it.'

'But it isn't just my single status I'm being tapped for, is it?' he threw back sourly.

'No,' she agreed, with another wry smile of appreciation at his wit, even in the face of all this horror. 'And you are going to have to…er…produce pretty potently, too, if you want this arrangement kept short-term.'

That had his gaze narrowing sharply on her studiedly impassive green eyes. He didn't like the tone of voice she had used but she didn't care that he didn't like it. She didn't *like* Alexander Doumas.

However, she would go to bed with him, if that was what it would take to get what she needed to gain from this dastardly deal.

'And what is the incentive that makes *you* agree to all of this?'

Mia didn't answer, wondering bleakly what his reaction would be if she told him the truth.

He was still standing by her father's drinks cabinet, his body tense and his expression tight with anger and contempt—for her, for himself, or even for both of them, she wasn't sure. And it really didn't matter because there was a whole lot more at stake here than his personal contempt— or even her own self-contempt, come to that.

Her father wanted a grandson to replace the son who had foolishly got himself killed in a car accident several months ago. Alexander Doumas had been chosen to father that grandson—Mia to be the vessel in which the poor child would be seeded.

This man's reasons for agreeing to any of this were based on his own personal ambitions. He wanted to get back the family island that lay somewhere off the Greek mainland, which his father had been forced to sell during the downfall of the family fortunes. Jack Frazier was the only person who could return it to him since he now owned the deeds to the island.

Mia, on the other hand, stood to gain far more than what amounted to a pile of ancient Greek rock. What was more,

she was quite prepared to do anything to complete her side
of the bargain she had made with her father.

'Like you, I get back something that once belonged to
me,' she murmured eventually.

'Am I to be told what?'

Her eyes clouded over, her mind shooting off to some
dark, dark place inside her that made her look so bleak and
saddened it actually threatened to breach his bristling contempt.

Then her lashes flickered, bringing her eyes back into
focus, and the bleak look was gone. 'No,' she replied, and
rose to her feet. 'That, I'm afraid, is none of your business.'

'It is if we are going to be man and wife,' he claimed.

'And are we?' Mia raised her sleek brows in counter-
challenge. 'Going to be man and wife?'

'Why me?' he asked suddenly. 'Why, if you did not
make the selection yourself, did your father set me up for
this?'

'Are you serious?' she gasped, her green eyes widening
in scathing incredulity. 'Last week you virtually undressed
me with your eyes right in front of him! The week before
that you invited me to spend the weekend in Paris with you
in front of a room full of people—including my father! And
there wasn't a person present who misunderstood what your
intentions were, Mr Doumas,' she informed him. 'You certainly were not offering to show the city sights to me!'

From the moment they'd met, he'd not even attempted
to hide the attraction he felt for her!

'You set yourself up for it!' she told him. 'I tried to head
you off, freeze you out as best as I could do in front of my
father. I even told you outright at one point that you were
playing with fire, coming anywhere near me! Did you take
any notice?' Her green eyes flashed. 'Did you hell!' she
snapped, ignoring the way his expression was growing
darker the more she threw at him. 'You just smiled an
amused little smile that told me you had the damned conceit

to think I was playing hard to get with you—and kept on coming on to me!

'And I'll tell you something else,' she continued, while he stood there, stiff-backed and riveted to the spot by what she was tossing at him. 'Until you started pursuing me, you weren't even up for consideration for this deal! But as soon as my father saw the way you looked at me you went right to the top of his carefully collected short-list of men fit to father his precious grandson! So, if you need to blame someone for this predicament you now find yourself in, blame yourself,' she suggested. 'You looked at me, you wanted me, you were offered me—on my father's terms.'

'In other words, your father is really your pimp,' he hit back.

Oh, very good, Mia grimly acknowledged. She'd cut into him, and he had cut right back.

'If you prefer to think of your future wife as a whore, then fine,' she parried. 'Though what that makes you doesn't really bear thinking about.'

He jerked as if she'd stabbed him—and so he damn well should! He might not like what he was being dealt here, but it didn't mean he could ride roughshod over her feelings!

'As it happens,' she tagged on, simply to twist the knife, 'you also had to pass several other tests before you qualified. You were younger than the other candidates on my father's list, as well as being more physically attractive—which was an important factor when my father was creating his grandson and heir,' she explained. 'But, most important of all, your family has a reputation for conceiving male children.' There hadn't been a female born to the Doumas line this century.

'And, of course, you were hungrier than the rest, not only for me,' she emphasized, 'but for your precious island.' And, therefore, so much easier to capture than the rest, was the bit she kept to herself.

But he took it as said. She saw that confirmed as his mouth took on a wryly understanding twist.

'And what happens to this—grandson and heir once he arrives in this world?' he asked next. 'Does your father come and snatch him from your breast an hour after his birth and expect me to forget I ever sired him?'

'Good heavens, no.' To his annoyance, she laughed again. 'My father has a real abhorrence of children in any shape or form.' Despite the laugh, her own bitter experience showed gratingly through. 'He simply desires a male heir to leave all his millions to. A legitimate male heir,' she added succinctly. 'I am afraid I can't go out and just get one from anywhere, if that's what you were going to suggest next...'

It had been a half-question, which his shrug completely dismissed. 'I'm not a complete fool,' he drawled. 'I would not suggest anything of the kind to you when it would mean my losing what I aim to gain from this.'

'And the child would lose a whole lot more, when you think about it,' Mia pointed out, referring to the size of Jack Frazier's well-known fortune. 'But I get full custody,' she announced with a lift of her chin that said she expected some kind of argument about it. 'That is not up for negotiation, Mr Doumas. It is my own condition before I will agree to any of this, and will be written into that contract my father mentioned to you.'

'Are you saying that I will have no control at all over this child?' he questioned sharply.

'Not at all,' Mia said. 'You will have all the rights any man would expect over his own son—so long as we stay married. But once the marriage is over I get full custody.'

'Why?'

Now there was a good question, Mia mused whimsically.

'I mean,' he qualified when she didn't answer him immediately, 'since you are making it damned obvious to me that you are no more enthusiastic about all of this than I am, why should you demand full custody of a child you don't really want in the first place?'

'I will *love* it,' she declared, 'no matter what his beginnings. I will *love* this child, Mr Doumas, not resent him, not look at him and despise him for who and what he means to me.'

'And you think I will?'

'I know you will,' she said with an absolute certainty. 'Men like you don't like to be constantly faced with their past failures.' She'd had experience of men of his calibre, after all—plenty of it. 'And agreeing to this deal most definitely represents a failure to you. So I get full custody,' she repeated firmly. 'Once the marriage is dissolved you will receive all the visitation rights legally allowed to you— if you still want them by then, of course,' she added, although her tone did not hold any optimism.

His eyes began to flash—the only warning she got that she had ignited something potentially dangerous inside him before he was suddenly standing right in front of her.

Her spine became erect, her eyelashes flickering warily as he pushed his angry face close to hers. 'You stand here with your chin held high and your beautiful eyes filled with a cold contempt for me, and dare to believe that you know exactly what kind of man I am—when you do not know me at all!' he rasped. 'For my son...' His hands came up to grip her shoulders. '*My son*,' he repeated passionately, 'will be *my* heir also!'

And it was a shock. Oh, not just the power of that possessiveness for something which was, after all, only a means to an end to him, but the effect his touch was having on her. It seemed to strike directly at the very heart of her, contracting muscles so violently that it actually squeezed the air from her tightened chest on a short, shaken gasp.

'*My son* will remain under *my* wing, no matter who—or what—his mother is!' he vowed. 'And if that means

trapping us both into a lifelong loveless marriage, then so
be it!'

'Are we?' Despite his anger, his biting grip, the bitter
hatred he was making no effort to hide, Mia's beautiful,
defiant eyes held his. 'Are we going to marry?'

His teeth showed, gleaming white and sharp and disturb-
ingly predatorial between the angry stretch of his lips, his
eyes like hard black pebbles that displayed a grinding distaste for both herself and the answer he was about to give
her.

'Yes,' he hissed with unmasked loathing. 'We will
marry. We will do everything expected of us to meet your
father's filthy terms! But don't,' he warned, 'let yourself
think for a moment that it is going to be a pleasure!'

'Then get your hands off me.' Coldly, she swiped his
hands away. 'And don't touch me again until it is absolutely necessary for us to touch!'

With that she turned and walked back to the window
where she stood, glaring outside at the lashing rain, while
she tried to get a hold on what was straining to erupt inside
her.

It didn't work. She could no more stop the words from
flowing than she could stop the rain outside from falling.
'You seem to think you have the divine right to stand there
and be superior to me. But you do not,' she muttered. 'You
have your price, just like the rest of us! Which makes you
no better than my father—no better than myself!'

'And what exactly is your price?' he challenged grimly.
'Give me one good reason why you are agreeing to all of
this and I might at least try to respect you for it!'

It was an appeal. An appeal that caught at her heart because, even through his anger, Mia could hear his genuine
desire for her to give him just cause for her own part in
this.

Her green eyes flashed then filmed over, as for a moment—for a tiny breathless space in time—the sheer

wretched truth to that question danced on the very edge of her tongue.

But she managed to smother the feeling, bite that awful truth down and keep it back, then spun to face him with her eyes made opaque by tears that had turned to ice.

'Money, of course,' she replied. 'What other price could there be?'

'Money...' he repeated, as though she had just confirmed every avaricious suspicion he'd held about her.

'On the day I present my father with a grandson I receive five million pounds as payment,' she went on. 'No better reason to agree to this—no worse than a man who can sell himself for a piece of land and a pile of ancient stone.'

He wasn't slow—he got her meaning. She was drawing a neat parallel between the two of them—or three people if she counted her father's willingness to give away a Greek island to get what he wanted out of this rotten deal.

'So make this a marriage for life if it suits you,' she defied him. 'I don't care. I will be wealthy in my own right and therefore independent of you no matter how long the marriage lasts! But we will soon know how strong your resolve is,' she added derisively, 'once the marriage is real and your sense of entrapment begins to eat away at you!'

'Entrapment?' he picked up on the word and shot it scornfully back at her. 'You naïvely believe I will feel trapped by this marriage? That I am prepared to change a single facet of my life to accommodate you or the vows we will make to each other?'

It was his turn to discharge a disdainful laugh, and Mia's turn to stiffen as his meaning began to sink in. 'I will change nothing!' he vowed. 'Not my way of life or my freedom to enjoy it wherever the mood takes me!'

His eyes were ablaze, anger and contempt for her lancing into her defiant face.

'I have a mistress in Athens with whom I am very happy,' he announced, using words like ice picks that he thrust into her. 'She will remain my mistress no matter what I have to do to fulfil my side of this filthy bargain! I will not be discreet.' he warned. 'I will not make any concessions to your pride while you live with me as my so-called wife! I will hate and despise you—and bed you with alacrity at regular intervals until this child of the devil is conceived, after which I will never touch you again!

'But,' he added harshly, 'if you truly believe I will also let you walk away with that child then you are living in a dream world because I will not!'

'Then the deal is off,' Mia instantly retaliated, using her father's tactics to make her own point.

After all, he hadn't given in to the big one—namely, agreeing to marry her and produce Jack Frazier's grandchild in what amounted to cold blood—without being desperate! And she would have her way in this if only because she had to glimpse some light at the end of this long dark tunnel or she knew she would not survive.

'Try telling your father that,' he derided, his eyes narrowing as her cheeks went white. 'You are afraid of him. I saw that from the first moment I set eyes on you.'

'And you want what only he can give you *more* than you want a child!' Mia countered. 'So I am telling *you* that you agree to my having full custody or the deal is off! This may also be a good moment for me to remind you of the shortlist of other names waiting to be called upon at a moment's notice,' she added, playing what she saw as her trump card.

To her immense satisfaction, his handsome face fell into harsh lines of raw frustration. 'You are as cold-blooded about this as your damned father!' he spat at her in disgust.

Mia said nothing, her chin up and eyes cool, her defiance in the face of his disdain so palpable it could almost be tasted in the air between them. Air that seemed to sing with enmity, picking at her flesh and tightening her throat as she watched him turn and stride angrily for the door.

'I will speak to my lawyers,' he said in a clipped voice

as he reached it, 'and let you know tomorrow what I decide.'

'F-fine,' Mia said, not quite managing to hide the sudden tremor of anxiety in her voice.

He heard it, and read it for exactly what it was. 'Your father is going to be bloody furious with you for not clinching this here and now, isn't he?' he taunted.

She merely shrugged one finely sculptured shoulder. 'My father knew my requirements before you arrived here. Why else do you think he left us alone like this when he actually had you so nicely caught in the bag?'

Take that, you nasty swine, she thought, her eyes gleaming with her own contempt.

One set of long, brown, lean fingers was gripping the brass doorhandle in preparation to open the door, but that final taunt had them sliding away again, and on a quiver of real alarm, which made her spine warily straighten, Mia watched him turn and begin to walk slowly towards her. Her heart began to hammer, her tongue cleaving to the dry roof of her mouth as he came to a halt mere inches away.

He was tall—taller than herself by several daunting inches. It meant she had to tilt her chin to maintain that most necessary eye-to-eye contact bitter adversaries always used as a weapon on each other.

His eyes were black, hard and narrowed, the finger he used to stroke a feather-light caress down the arched column of her throat an electric provocation that had her teeth gritting behind the firm set of her lips as she fought to stop herself from flinching away from him.

'You know...' he murmured, super-light, super-soft, 'you are in real danger of provoking me one step too far. I wonder why that is?'

'I d-don't know what you're talking about,' she said tremulously, feeling that trailing finger make its electrifying journey back up her throat again.

'No?' he said quizzically.

Then he showed her exactly what he meant as that taunting finger suddenly became a hand that cupped her jaw then tilted her head as his mouth came down to capture hers.

It was not a passionate kiss or even a punishing one. He simply crushed her slightly parted lips against his own, tasted her, using his tongue to lick a lazy passage along the vulnerable curve of her mouth, then straightened, his eyes still like dark glass as they gazed into her own rather startled ones.

'W-why did you do that?' she gasped.

'Why do you think?' he replied mockingly. 'I wanted to know if I would taste the acid that drips constantly from your lips. It wasn't there,' he softly confided. 'In fact, you tasted so sweet I think I will have to taste you again...'

And he did, that warning all she had before he was crushing her lips again, only this time his exploring tongue was sliding sinuously along the edge of her own, and as she released a protesting gasp his free hand snaked round her waist and pulled her against the long lean length of his body—a body she could feel already tightening with an arousal that actually shocked her.

But what shocked her more was the way her own senses went absolutely haywire, slinging out all kinds of demands that had her simmering from head to toe. The static-packed build-up of sensual excitement set her quivering all over and it was an effort not to give in.

What was the matter with her? she wondered deliriously. She didn't even like this man!

Yet she was on fire already, and she had to admit he was good. He seduced her mouth with an expertise that had her groaning, the splay of his hands across her body holding her trapped so he could move against her in a blatant demonstration of what the friction between their two bodies was doing to him.

To her horror, her own inner thighs began to pulse in hungry answer, her mouth quivered, her breathing quick-ened and her hands came up to cling to his shoulders as, on another helpless groan, her defences finally collapsed, and she was kissing him back with a passion that held her totally captivated.

It was raw and it was hot and it was so utterly basic that his deep-throated laugh of triumph against her clinging mouth had to be the worst humiliation she had ever experienced.

'Now this is a surprise,' he murmured silkily as he drew away. 'I knew our sparring was arousing me, but I did not realise it was having the same effect upon you. That adds a little spice to my final decision, does it not?'

Mia took a shaky step backwards, her trembling fingers falling from his shoulders and her cheeks blooming with shock and a dreadful consternation.

'Lie back and mentally switch off?' He mocked her earlier remark. 'I think you will be doing a whole lot more than that, Mia Frazier.'

'I never said I was frigid,' she shot back stiffly.

'But your father must think you are or why else does he believe he has to pay to get a man to bed you?'

'Not just any man, but the man of his own choice!' Her chin was up again and, despite the quivers still shaking her body, her eyes still managed to spit out defiance. 'Please remember that while you make your decision—you are not my personal choice. I am simply willing to do anything for that five millions pounds.'

Which was about as good as a slap in the face for him. He stepped right away from her, his expression so utterly disgusted that she almost—almost—wished the words unsaid.

'I will call you with my decision tomorrow,' he said abruptly as he moved back to the door.

'It's my father you will be dealing with, not me.'

'You,' he repeated. 'I will deal personally with *you*. Your father will be dealt with through my lawyers.'

CHAPTER TWO

MIA was staring out of the study window again when her father entered the room. She had just watched Alexander Doumas take off down the driveway with enough angry force to forge a vacuum through the storm still raging outside. There were tears in her eyes, though she didn't know why—unless those tears had something to do with the awful person she had been forced to play here today who bore no resemblance to the real Mia Frazier.

'Well, how did it go?'

'He has until tomorrow to agree to my terms or the deal is off,' she replied, without bothering to turn.

In the small silence that followed she sensed her father's frown of irritation. 'Don't spoil this for me, Mia,' he warned her very grimly, 'or you will be spoiling it for yourself.'

'I was taught by an expert.' Mia's smile was bleak. 'He will come around to my way of thinking simply because he has no choice.'

'Neither do you.'

'He doesn't know that, though.'

'Ah.' Jack Frazier lowered himself into the chair behind his desk with a sigh of satisfaction. 'You didn't tell him.'

'You warned me not to.'

'So, what does he think I am holding up as your incentive to agree to all of this?'

'I get five million pounds from you on the day I produce your grandson,' she informed him.

'Five million?' he grimaced. 'A nice round figure.'

'I thought so, too,' Mia agreed. 'It makes me a really expensive whore, don't you think?'

'You've always been a whore, darling,' Jack Frazier murmured insultingly. 'Expensive or cheap, a whore is still a whore. Tell Mrs Leyton I'm ready for some coffee now that the Greek has gone.'

Just like that. His low opinion of her stated, he was now calmly changing the subject.

Moving over to the desk, Mia lifted the internal phone which would connect her to the kitchen and held tightly locked inside herself the few choice replies that rattled around her brain regarding this man whom she was so ashamed to have to call her father.

Which was why neither Jack Frazier nor Alexander Doumas would ever have any control over her son. They could lay legal claims as mere blood relatives—she didn't mind that. They could even leave him every penny they possessed when they both decided to make this world a better place by leaving it.

But they would not have any control over who and what her son grew into. She already had in her possession her father's written agreement to that. And when tomorrow came she would be getting the same written agreement from Mr Doumas.

And how could she feel so sure about that? Because she had his measure. She had watched her father carefully mark it when he got the arrogant Greek to agree to any of this in the first place. If Alexander Doumas was prepared to wed and bed a woman just to get his hands on his old family pile then he would give away his first-born child also.

'If he surprises us both and doesn't give in to your terms,' her father posed quietly, 'what will you do then?'

'Wait until you come up with someone who will agree.'

His eyes began to gleam. 'The next on the list is Marcus Sidcup,' he reminded her silkily. 'Can you honestly bring yourself to let him touch you, Mia?'

Marcus Sidcup was a grotesque little man several years

older than her father who turned her stomach every time she set eyes on him. 'I'm a whore,' she replied. 'Whores can't be too picky. I'll close my eyes and think nice thoughts, like what to wear at your funeral.'

He laughed. Her opinion of him had never mattered simply because she didn't matter to him, the main reason being that she reminded him too much of his dead wife's many infidelities. Her brother Tony's conception had been just as suspect as her own, but because he had been male her father had been willing to accept him as his own. Mia being female, though, her paternity was an entirely different matter.

'If all goes well with Mr Doumas tomorrow,' she tossed in as a mere aside, 'I intend to go and visit Suzanna at school. She will need to know why I won't be around much for the next year or so.'

'You will tell her only what she needs to be told,' her father commanded sharply.

'I'm not a complete fool,' Mia replied. 'I have no wish to raise her hopes, but neither do I want her to think that I've deserted her.'

'She will be making no trips to visit you in Greece, either,' Jack Frazier warned her, 'so don't go all soft and try to placate her with promises that I might agree to it because I will not.'

Mia never for one moment thought that he would. Her eyes bleak and her heart aching for that small scrap of a seven-year-old who had seen even less of this man's love than she herself had, she walked out of the room before she was tempted to say something really nasty.

She couldn't afford to be nasty. She couldn't afford to get her father's back up, not when she was this close to achieving her own precious dream.

And she couldn't afford to lose Alexander Doumas either, she admitted heavily to herself, because no matter how much she despised him for being what he was he was her best option in this deal she had made with her father.

Pray to God he was as hungry as her father claimed he was, was the final thought she allowed herself to have that day on the subject.

The call came early the next morning just as Mia was emerging from her usual twenty laps of their indoor swimming pool. Mrs Leyton came to inform her that a Mr Doumas was waiting to speak to her on the phone. Wringing the water out of her hair as she walked across the white tiles, she went to the pool phone extension and picked up the receiver.

'Yes?' she said coolly.

'Yes,' he threw right back with a grim economy of words that showed every bit of his angry distaste. 'Be here at my offices at noon,' he commanded. 'My lawyers will have something ready for you to sign by then.'

Click. The phone went dead. Mia stood and grimaced at the inert piece of plastic, then ruefully replaced it on its wall rest.

At noon exactly she presented herself in the foyer of the very luxurious Doumas Corporation. Dressed in a severely tailored black pin-striped wool suit and plain white blouse, she looked the epitome of cool business elegance with her long, silky, copper hair neatly contained, as usual, in a knot high on her head and her make-up as understated as everything always was about her.

But, then, Mia Frazier did not need to make dress statements to look absolutely stunning. She was tall and incredibly slender, with legs so long that even a conservative knee-length skirt couldn't diminish their sensational impact.

Her skin was wonderful, so clear and smooth and white that it made the ocean greenness of her eyes stand out in startling contrast and the natural redness of her small heart-shaped mouth look lush and inviting and unwittingly sensual.

Add to all of that the kind of feminine curves that promised perfection beneath the severe clothing, and men stopped and stared when she walked into a room—as if they could recognise by instinct that beneath the cloak of cool reserve hid an excitingly sensual woman.

Alexander Doumas had been one man who had looked and instinctively seen her like that. One evening, a month ago, he had been standing with a group of people at a charity function when Mia had walked into the room on her father's arm.

He had been aware of who she was, of course, and who her father was, and how important Jack Frazier was to his reasons for being in London at all. But, still, he had taken one look at Jack's beautiful daughter and had made the most colossal tactical error of his life, by deciding he would like to mix business with a bit of pleasure.

It had been his downfall, which was how Mia liked to remember that moment. He had seen, he had desired and had done nothing whatsoever to hide that desire from either herself or her watching father. Maybe he had even seen his own actions as a way to ingratiate himself with Jack Frazier. Flatter the daughter to impress the father—that kind of thing—she had never really been sure.

Whatever, he had signed his own death warrant that very same evening when he had detached himself from his friends so he could come and introduce himself to Jack Frazier. His words might have been directed at her father but his eyes had all but consumed Mia.

In her own defence, Mia had tried to head him off before he had sunk himself too deeply into her father's clutches. She'd remained cool, aloof, indifferent to every soft-voiced compliment he had paid her—had tried to freeze him out when he wouldn't be frozen out.

For her own reasons. Alexander Doumas was one of the most attractive men she had ever laid eyes on, but for what she already knew her father was planning for her the Greek was just too much of everything. Too young, too dynamic, too sensually charismatic. Too obviously used to handling power, and just too confident in his own ability to win—both in the boardroom and the bedroom.

She needed a weaker man, a man with less of an aura of strength about him—a man with whom she could carry out her father's wishes and then walk away, spiritually un-scathed, once the dastardly deal was done.

She certainly did not need a man who could make her heart race just by settling his lazily admiring dark eyes on her, or one whose lightest touch on her arm could make her flesh come alive with all kinds of unwanted sexual mur-murings. A man whose voice made her toes curl and whose smile rendered her breathless. In other words, a man with all the right weapons to hurt her. She had been hurt enough in her life by men of Alexander Doumas's calibre.

She'd tried very hard to freeze him out during the last few weeks when her father made sure they were thrown together at every opportunity, but the stupid, stubborn man refused to be pushed away.

Now he was paying the consequences—or was about to pay them, Mia amended as she paused just inside the foyer.

The Doumas name had once been connected exclusively with oil and shipping, but since Alexander Doumas had taken over the company had diversified into the far more lucrative business of holidays and leisure. Now the name was synonymous with all that was the best and most lux-urious in accommodation across the world. Their hotel chain and fleet of holiday cruise liners were renowned for their taste and splendour.

And all in ten years, Mia mused appreciatively as she set herself moving across the marble floor towards the recep-tion desk. Before that the Doumas family had been facing bankruptcy and, from what her father had told her, had only just managed to stave it off by selling virtually everything they possessed.

Alexander Doumas had managed to hang on to one

cruise liner and a small hotel in Athens, which no one had actually known the family owned until he had begun to delve into their assets.

But that one cruise liner and hotel had been all that had been needed for the man to begin the rebuilding of an empire. Now he had by far outstripped what the family had once had, and the only goal left in his corporate life was regaining the family island.

Quite how her father had come by the island Mia had no idea. It was his way, though, to pick the bones clean of those in dire straits. He bought at rock-bottom prices from the absolutely desperate then moved in his team of business experts, who would pull the ailing company back into good health before he sold it on for the kind of profit that made one's hair curl.

Some things he didn't bother to sell on—like the house they lived in now, which he'd acquired for a snip from a man who'd lost everything in the last stockmarket crash. Jack Frazier had simply moved into it himself as it was in one of the most prestigious areas of London. The yacht and the plane had been acquired the same way, and of course the tiny Greek island that he'd held onto because—whatever else her father was that she hated and despised—he was astute.

He would have watched Alexander Doumas begin to rebuild the family fortunes. He would have known that the proud Greek would one day want his island back, and he had simply waited until the price was right for him to offer it back.

'I am here to see Mr Doumas,' Mia informed the young woman behind the reception desk. 'My name is Mia Frazier.'

'Oh, yes, Miss Frazier.' The girl didn't even need to glance down at the large appointment book she had open in front of her. 'You'll need to take the lift to the top floor, where someone will meet you.'

With a murmured word of thanks, Mia moved off as gracefully as always, and so well controlled that no one would have known how badly her insides were shaking or that her throat was tight with a mixture of dread and horror at what she was allowing herself to walk into. Yet, abhor herself as she undoubtedly did, her footsteps did not falter nor did her resolve. The stakes were too high and the rewards at the end of it too great to allow any room for doubt.

She walked into a waiting lift and pressed the button for the top floor without a pause. She kept her chin firm and her teeth set behind steady lips as she took that journey upwards, her clear green eyes fixing themselves on the framed water-colour adorning the back wall of the lift.

It was a painting of the most beautiful villa, set on the side of a hill and surrounded by trees. The walls were white, the roof terra-cotta and the garden a series of flower-strewn terraces sweeping down to a tiny bay where a primitively constructed old wooden jetty protruded into deeper, darker waters and a simple fishing boat stood tied alongside it.

What really caught her interest was the tiny horseshoe-shaped clearing in a cluster of trees to the left of the house. It seemed to be a graveyard. She could just make out the shapes of simple crosses amongst a blaze of colourful flowers.

A strange detail to put in such a pretty picture, she mused frowningly. *Vision* it was simply titled. Whose vision? she wondered. That of the man she was here to see or the artist who had painted it?

'Miss Frazier?'

The slightly accented cool male voice brought her swinging round to discover in surprise that not only had the lift come to a stop without her realising it, but the doors had opened and she was now being spoken to by a tall, dark, olive-skinned stranger. A stranger who was eyeing her so coldly that she had to assume he knew exactly why she was here today.

'Yes,' she confirmed, with a tilt of her chin that defied his right to judge her.

Something flashed in his eyes—surprise at her clear challenge? Or maybe it was more basic than that, she suggested to herself as she watched his dark eyes dip in a very male assessment of her whole body, as if he had some kind of right to check her out like a prime piece of saleable merchandise!

Which is exactly what you are, Mia reminded herself with her usual brutal honesty.

'And you are?' she countered in her crispest, coldest upper-class English, bringing those roving eyes flicking back up to clash with the clear green challenge reflected in her own.

His ears darkened. It was such a boyish response to being caught, blatantly staring, that she almost found it in her to laugh. Only… It suddenly hit her that there was something very familiar about this young man's features.

'I am Leonadis Doumas,' he informed her. 'My brother is this way, if you would follow me…'

Ah, the brother. She smiled a rueful smile. No wonder he looked familiar. The same eyes, the same physique— though without the same dynamic impact as his brother. Perhaps he was more handsome in a purely aesthetic way but, by the way his colour remained heightened as she followed him towards a pair of closed doors, she judged he lacked his brother's cool sophistication.

Leonadis Doumas paused, then knocked lightly on one of the closed doors, before pushing it open, and Mia used that moment to take a deep breath to prepare herself for what was to come next.

It didn't help much, and a fresh attack of nerves almost had her turning to run in the opposite direction before this thing was taken right out of her hands.

But, as she had told Alexander Doumas only yesterday, her father did not deal in uncertainties. He knew she would go ahead with this, just as he had known that Alexander Doumas would go ahead with it, no matter how much it made him despise himself.

Leonadis Doumas was murmuring something in Greek. Mia heard the now-familiar deep tones of his brother in reply before the younger man stepped aside to let her pass him.

She did so reluctantly, half expecting to find herself walking into a room full of grey-suited lawyers. Instead, she found herself facing the only other person present in the room. Alexander was sitting at his desk, with the light from the window catching the raven blackness of his neatly styled hair.

Behind her the door closed. She glanced back to find that Leonadis had gone. Mia's stomach muscles clenched into a tight knot of tension as she turned back to face the man with whom—soon—she was going to have to lie and share the deepest intimacy.

'Very businesslike,' he drawled. 'I believe it's called power dressing. But I feel I should warn you that it's lost on me.'

Startled by the unexpected choice of his first attack, Mia glanced down at her severely tailored suit, with its modest-length skirt and prim white blouse, and only then realised that he had completely misinterpreted why she was dressed like this.

Not that it mattered, she decided as her chin came back up and she levelled her cool green eyes on him. She had dressed like this because she was going on to Suzanna's very strict boarding school directly from here, where strait-laced conservatism was insisted upon from family and pupils alike.

'When you marry me,' he went on, 'I will expect some-

thing more...womanly. I find females in masculine attire a
real turn-off.'

'*If* I marry you,' Mia corrected, and made herself walk
forward until only the width of his desk was separating
them. 'Your brother looks like you,' she observed as a mere
aside.

For some reason, the remark seemed to annoy him.
'Wondering if your father tapped the wrong brother?' he
asked. 'Leon is nine years younger than me, which places
him just about in your own age group, I suppose. But he
is also very much off-limits, as far as you are concerned,'
he added with a snap that made his words into a threat.

'I have no inclination to so much as touch him,' she
countered, smiling slightly because she knew then that big
brother must have noticed and correctly interpreted the reason his younger brother was looking so warm about the
ears. 'Though, you never know,' she couldn't resist adding,
'it may be worth my while to look into whether he would
be a better bet than you before I commit myself.'

Again there was the hint of anger. 'Leon is already very
much married to a wonderful creature he adores,' he said
abruptly. 'Which makes him of absolutely no use to you.'

'Ah, married.' She sighed. 'Shame. Then it looks as if
you will have to do.'

With that little ego-deflater, she lowered herself into a
chair and waited for his next move.

To her surprise, his mouth twitched, appreciation for her
riposte suddenly glinting in his eyes. He was no one's fool.
He knew without vanity that he was a better, more attractive, more sensually appealing man than his younger, less
dynamic brother.

'A contract my lawyers have drawn up this morning,' he
announced, reaching out with a long fingered hand for a
document of several pages which he slid across the desk
towards her. 'I suggest you read that thoroughly before you
sign it.'

'I have every intention of doing so,' she said, picking up the contract. She proceeded to ignore him while she immersed herself in its detail.

It was a comprehensive document, which set out point by point the guidelines by which this so-called marriage of theirs would proceed. In a way, Mia supposed the first part read more like a prenuptial agreement than a business contract, with its declarations on how small an allowance he would be giving her on a monthly basis and what little she could expect from him if the marriage came to an end—which was a pittance, though she wasn't surprised by that.

The man believed she would be a wealthy woman in her own right once all this was over. It suited her to continue to let him go on thinking that way so she didn't care that he was offering her nothing.

It was only on the third page that things began to get nasty. She would live where he wanted her to live, it stipulated. She would sleep where he wanted her to sleep. If she went out at all she would never do so without one of his designated people as a companion.

She would be available at all times for sex on his demand…

Mia felt his eyes on her, following, she was sure, line by line as she read. Her cheeks wanted to redden, but she refused to allow them to, her lips drawing in on themselves because it seemed so distasteful to add such a clause when, after all, they were only marrying because of the sex, which was necessary to make babies.

She would conduct herself at all times in a way which made her actions as his wife above reproach, she grimly read on. She would not remark on his own personal life outside their marriage, and she accepted totally that he intended to maintain a mistress…

The fact that several slick lawyers were privy to all of this, as well as the person who had typed it, made her want to cringe in horror.

In anticipation of her falling pregnant, she would not step off Greek soil without his permission during her pregnancy. The child must be born in Greece and registered as Greek. In the event of the marriage irretrievably breaking down, yes, she would get full custody of their child, she was relieved to read.

Then came his own proviso to that concession, and it made her heart sink. It had to be *his* decision that the marriage must end. If Mia walked out on the marriage of her own volition then she did so knowing she would be forfeiting full custody...

'I can't agree to that,' she protested.

'You are not being given a choice,' he replied, leaning back in his chair yet reading with her word for word of the contract. 'I did warn you that I would not relinquish control of my own son and heir. I have the right to safeguard myself against that contingency, just as you have the right to safeguard yourself against my walking out on you. So it is covered both ways by that particular clause.

'If I decide I cannot bear having you as my wife any longer, then I get rid of you, knowing I will be relinquishing all rights to our child. If you decide the same thing then you, too, will relinquish all rights over him. I think that is fair, don't you?'

Did she? She had a horrible feeling she was being scuppered here, though the logic of his argument gave her no clue as to where. And, in the end, did it matter? she then asked herself. She had no intention of marrying any man ever again after this. If Alexander Doumas wanted to tie himself to this wife for life, let him.

'Is there anything else you want to add to this?' he asked, once she'd read the contract to the end without further comment.

Mia shook her head. Whatever she felt she needed to safeguard for herself would be done privately with her own lawyer in the form of a last will and testament.

Getting to her feet, she picked up her handbag. 'I'll let my father look at this then get back to you,' she informed him coolly.

'No.'

In the act of turning towards the door Mia paused, her neat head twisting to let her eyes clash with his for the first time since this interview had begun. Her heart stopped beating for a moment and her porcelain-like skin chilled at the uncompromising grimness she saw in those dark eyes.

'This is between you and me,' he insisted. 'Whatever is agreed between your father and myself—or even your father and yourself—will be kept completely separate from this contract. But you decide now and sign now or—to use your own words—the deal is off.'

'I would have to be a complete fool if I didn't get this checked out by someone professional before I put my signature to it,' she protested.

'You want a professional here? Give me the name of your lawyer and I will have him here in half an hour,' he said. 'But I think it only fair to warn you first that I refuse to alter one single word on that contract, no matter what advice he offers you. So...' A shrug threw the ball back into her court.

Well, Mia, what are you going to do? she asked herself as she stood, gazing at this man with his intractable expression that so reminded her of her father.

She shivered. He was contemptuous of who she was and what she was, indifferent to what she felt or even *if* she felt. He was ready, she was sure, to make her pay in every way he could, for bringing him down to this.

Oh, yes, she thought grimly. Just like her father. Every bit the same kind of man. Which made her wonder suddenly if that was why Jack Frazier had chosen Alexander Doumas in the first place. Was it because he saw in this man a more than adequate successor to himself as her tormentor?

'Are you at last beginning to wonder if five million pounds is worth the kind of purgatory you are about to embark upon if you marry me?' this particular tormentor prodded silkily.

'No,' she said, dropping both the contract and her handbag back onto the desk. 'I was merely trying to decide whether it was worthwhile calling your bluff,' she explained, 'but, since I have another pressing engagement, I've decided not to bother haggling with you. So...' Her chin came up, her green eyes as cool and as indifferent as they had ever been. 'Where do I sign?'

It took the whole of the long drive into Bedfordshire to pull her utterly ragged senses back into some semblance of calm because from the moment she'd agreed to sign his rotten contract the meeting had sunk to an all-time low in the humiliation stakes.

He hadn't liked her consigning him to second place behind whatever engagement she had, she knew that. It had been exactly why she had said it, hadn't it?

But what had come afterwards had made her wish she'd kept her reckless mouth shut. Punishment was the word that came to mind. He'd punished her by introducing her to the two lawyers he'd called in to witness their signatures as 'the woman who is this desperate to bear my child' as he'd tossed the contract towards them to sign.

It had been cruel and unnecessary but he hadn't cared. The way his hard eyes had mocked the hot colour that swept up her cheeks had shown he'd even enjoyed seeing her so discomfited.

Then had come the final humiliation once the lawyers had been dismissed again.

The kiss.

Her whole body quivered in appalled reaction, her lips still throbbing in memory of the ruthless way he had devoured them. He'd done it so cavalierly, coming around his

desk in what she'd foolishly believed had been an intention
to escort her politely to the door. What he'd actually done
had been to reach out and pull her into his arms then capture her mouth with the same grim precision he had
achieved the day before.

Only this time he had taken that kiss a whole lot further,
Staking his claim, she realised now. Staking his claim on
a piece of property he had just bought, by deepening the
kiss with all the casual expertise of a man who knew exactly how to make a woman's senses catch fire at his will.

And she had caught fire—that was the truly humiliating
part of it. She had just stood there in his arms and had gone
up like a Roman candle! She'd quivered and groaned and
clung to his mouth, as though her very survival had depended on it.

Where had her pride been? Her self-control? Her determination to remain aloof from him, no matter what he did
to her?

What he did to you? her mind screamed jeeringly back
at her. What about what you did to him?

'No...' The word escaped as a wretched groan from anguished lips, and she had to slow the car down because her
vision was suddenly misted. Misted by terrible visions of
her fingers clutching at him—at his nape, and his hair—
holding him to her when she should have been pushing him
away!

He'd muttered something—she could still hear that
driven groan echoing inside her shell-shocked head. Could
still feel the burning pressure of his body against hers, of
buttons parting, of flesh preening to the pleasure of his
touch and the sudden flare of a powerful male arousal, the
crush of his arms as he'd pressed her even closer.

It had been awful. They'd devoured each other like hungry animals, so fevered by desire that when he'd suddenly
let go of her she'd staggered backwards with flushed skin
and dazed eyes, her pulsing mouth parted and gasping for

air as she'd stood there, staring blankly at him as he'd
swung away from her.

'Cover yourself,' he'd rasped.

A shudder of self-revulsion shot through her, making her
foot slip on the accelerator when she saw in her mind's eye
what he must have seen as he'd stood there, glowering at
her, with the desk once more between them.

Her jacket, her blouse—even her fine lacy bra—gaping
wide to reveal the fullness of her breasts in tight, tingling
distension!

'I can't believe you did that,' she whispered, turning her
back to him while useless fingers fumbled in their attempts
to put her clothing back in order.

'Why not?' he countered flatly. 'It is what you signed
up for.'

Humiliation almost suffocated her. 'I hate you,' she
choked.

'But I don't think you're going to find the sex a problem,
do you?'

Recognising her own taunt from yesterday being flung
right back at her, she shuddered again.

'Not surprising, really,' he continued remorselessly,
'when rumour has it that you were a bit of a raver in your
teens…'

Her teens? She went very still. The fact that he knew
about her wild teenage rebellion was enough to keep her
ready tongue locked inside her kiss-numbed mouth.

'Well, let's get one more thing straight before you leave
this room,' he continued very grimly. 'You will behave like
a lady while you belong to me. There will be no wild par-
ties, no rave-ups. No sleeping around when the mood happens to take you.'

'I'm not like that.' She was constrained to defend herself.

'Now? Who knows?' he said derisively. 'While you are
married to me? No chance. I want to know that the child
you will eventually carry is my child,' he vowed, 'or you

will be wishing you'd never heard the name Doumas! Now, pull yourself together before you walk out of this room,' he concluded dismissively. 'We will marry in three days' time.'

'Three days?' she gasped, spinning round to stare at him. 'But—'

It was as far as she got. 'Three days,' he repeated. 'I see no reason to delay—especially when I know what a receptive little thing you're going to be in my bed,' he added silkily at her white-faced shock. 'The sooner we get this show on the road the sooner I get you pregnant, and you get your five million pounds and I get back what should be mine.'

He meant his island, of course. The stupid bit of Greek rock he was prepared to sell his soul for—or, at the very least, his DNA. The man had no concept of which was really more important. She could have told him, but she didn't.

In fact, she wanted him to go right on believing that his island was worth more to him than his DNA. That way she could finally beat him, which was really all that mattered to her.

The only thing she could do now was think ahead. A long way ahead to a time when—God willing—the awful man would grow tired of her and eventually let her go.

Suzanna was heart-achingly pleased to see her. But the seven-year-old broke down and wept her heart out when Mia told her gently that she was going away for a while.

Pulling her onto her lap, she let the little girl weep herself dry. Heaven knew, there were too few moments when she could give her emotions free rein like this.

'It will only be for a year or two,' she murmured soothingly, 'and I will come and see you as often as I can.'

'But not like you do now,' the child protested, 'because Greece is a long, long way away! And it's going to mean that I will have to spend the school holidays alone with Daddy!'

The alarm that prospect caused the poor child cut deeply into Mia's heart. 'Mrs Leyton will be there for you,' Mia reminded her. 'You like her, don't you?'

'But I can't bear not having you there, too, Mia!' she sobbed. 'He h-hates me! You know he does because he hates you too!'

Mia sighed and hugged the child closer because she knew she couldn't even lie and deny the charge. Jack Frazier did hate them both. He had poured what bit of love he had ever had in him into their brother, Tony. With Tony gone, their father had just got more and more resentful of their very existence.

'Look,' she murmured suddenly out of sheer guilt and desperation, even though her father's warning was ringing shrilly in her ears, 'I promise to call you once a week so we can talk on the telephone.'

'You promise?' the child whispered.

'I promise,' Mia vowed.

She hugged the thin little body tightly to her because it wasn't fair—not to herself, not to Suzanna. May God forgive me, she prayed silently, for deserting her like this.

'I love you, my darling,' she whispered thickly. 'You are and always will be the most important thing in my life.'

She got back to the house after dark, feeling limp and empty.

'Your father's flown off to Geneva,' Mrs Leyton informed her. 'He said to tell you not to expect him back before you leave here. Why are you leaving here?'

The poor old lady looked so shocked that it took the very last dregs of Mia's strength to drag up another set of explanations. 'I'm going to be living in Greece for a year or two,' she said.

'With that Greek fellow that was here the other day?'

'Yes.' Her tired mouth tightened. 'We are—getting married,'

'And your father agrees?' Mrs Layton sounded stunned.

'He—arranged it,' Mia said, with a smile that wasn't a smile but more a grimace of irony. Then she added anxiously, 'You'll keep an eye on Suzanna for me, won't you, while I'm away?'

'You should be staying here to do that yourself,' the housekeeper said sternly.

'I can't, Cissy.' At last the tears threatened to fall. 'Not for the next year or so, anyway. Please don't quiz me about it—just promise me you'll watch her and keep my father away from her as much as you can!'

'Don't I always?' the housekeeper snapped, but her old eyes were shrewd. Mia had a suspicion that she knew exactly what was going on. 'That Greek chap has been on the telephone, asking for you, umpteen times today. He didn't sound very pleased that you weren't here to take his calls.'

'Well, that's his hard luck.' Mia dismissed Alexander Doumas and all he represented. 'I'm tired. I'm going to bed.'

'And if he rings again?'

'Tell him to leave a message then go to hell,' she said, walking away up the stairs and into her room where she stripped herself with the intention of having a shower. But it couldn't even wait that long and the next moment she had thrown herself down on her bed and was sobbing brokenly into her pillow, just as Suzanna had sobbed in her arms this afternoon.

CHAPTER THREE

'WHERE the hell have you been for the last three days?'

Mia's insides jumped, her eyes jerking sideways to skitter briefly over the dark-suited figure seated next to her in the car.

Alexander looked grim-faced and tense. She didn't blame him. She felt very much the same way herself, hence her jumping insides, because he had actually spoken to her directly for the first time since that dreadful marriage ceremony had taken place.

'I had things to do,' she replied, her nervous fingers twisting the unfamiliar gold ring that now adorned her finger.

'And I had things I needed to check with you,' he bit back.

'Mrs Leyton answered all your questions,' Mia parried coolly. Hadn't it occurred to him that she was the one who was having to uproot her whole life for this? He'd given her three days to do it in—three damn days!

But that hadn't been the real reason she had refused to accept any of his phone calls. She'd needed these last few days to get a hold on herself, to come to terms with what had erupted between them in his office.

It hadn't worked. She was still horrified by it all, frightened by it all.

'Well, fob me off like that again, and you won't like the consequences,' he muttered.

I already don't like them, she thought heavily, but just shrugged a slender shoulder and kept her gaze fixed firmly on the slowly changing scenery beyond the limousine window.

And it was strange, really, she mused, but here she sat, married to this man. He had kissed her twice, ruthlessly violated her sexual privacy once, had insulted her and shown her his contempt and disgust in so many ways during their two short interviews that it really did not bear thinking about. Yet during all of that, including the brief civil ceremony which had taken place this morning with no family present on either side, not even his own brother, Leon—which had acted as a clear message in itself to Mia—their eyes had barely ever clashed.

Oh, they'd looked at each other, she conceded drily. But it had been a careful dance as to when he looked or she looked, but they had not allowed themselves to look at the same time.

Why? she asked herself. Because neither of them were really prepared to accept that they were actually doing this. It went so against the grain of civilised society that even the Greek in him must be appalled at the depths to which he had allowed himself to sink in the name of desire.

Not sexual desire but the desire for property.

'Why the smile?'

Ah, she thought, his turn to look at me. 'I was wondering if my father was enjoying a glass of champagne somewhere in Geneva,' she lied. 'Celebrating his success in getting us both this far.'

'He isn't in Geneva,' he said, watching impassively as her slender spine straightened. 'He has been staying with his mistress in Knightsbridge since I signed his bloody contract. I presume he wanted to keep out of your way in case you started asking awkward questions about what he actually got me to sign in the end.'

Her chin turned slowly, supported by a neck that was suddenly very tense, her wary eyes flickering over his face without really focusing before she lowered them again. There was something—something snake-like in the way he had imparted all that which made her feel slightly sick inside.

'The two of you can't possibly have agreed anything else to do with me without my say-so,' she declared rather shakily.

'True. We didn't.' He relieved her mind with his confirmation. 'But we did discuss the fact that you have a younger sister...'

Oh, no. She closed her eyes, her heart sinking to her stomach. Her father would not have told this man about Suzanna, surely?

'He wanted me to know what a bad influence you are on the child,' that hateful voice continued, while Mia's mind had shot off in another direction entirely. 'Therefore, while you are with me you are to have no contact with—Suzanna, isn't it? Apparently, you are very jealous of her and can, if allowed to, make her young life a misery...'

So that was how her father was playing it. Her eyes bleak and bitter behind her lowered lids, Mia pressed her lips together and said nothing. No contact with Suzanna would keep her striving to make the grandson her father wanted so badly. No contact with Suzanna was meant as a warning—do your job or forget all about her.

'Is that why he married you off to the highest bidder?' her new husband continued remorselessly. 'To get you right out of your sister's life?'

'You didn't bid for me—you were *bought!*' She hit back at him. 'For the specific purpose of producing my father's precious grandson! So, if the reputation for making sons in your family lets you down,' she finished shakily, 'make sure you don't blame me for the mistake!'

He should have been angry. Heavens, she'd said it all to make him angry! But all he did was huff a lazy laugh of pure male confidence.

'My mother had three sons and my grandmother five. I don't think I need worry on that score. And,' he added as he shifted his lean bulk to glance out of the car window, 'that was not the point I was trying to make. I was simply letting you know that I now know why your father was willing to pay you five million pounds to get you out of his life.'

'Plus a Greek island,' Mia added. 'Please don't forget the island—how much is that worth in cold, hard cash?'

His face hardened at the reminder, the link she was making between them so clear that even he, for all his arrogance, could not deny it was there.

'We have arrived,' he said, bringing an end to the conversation.

Sure enough, the car pulled to a stop and Mia looked out to find they had come to one of the private airfields just outside London. A gleaming white Gulfstream jet sat glinting in the weak winter sunlight, the Doumas logo painted in gold on its side.

Ten minutes after that Mia found herself ensconced in luxurious cream leather—alone.

Her new husband, she discovered, was apparently going to fly them wherever they were going. He disappeared into the cockpit the moment they boarded and she did not set eyes on him again until they landed—in Greece she had to assume because no one had bothered to inform her.

He came striding into the main cabin minus his jacket and silk tie. He looked different somehow, less formal, but all the more intimidating for it.

Male—that was the word that suddenly came to mind. He looked more aggressively male than he had done before. Once again she lowered her eyes before he could glimpse what she was thinking, and bent to pick up her jacket which she, too, had discarded during the flight.

So she didn't see the way his eyes narrowed on the firm thrust of her breasts, outlined by the close fit of her clinging white top. She didn't see those eyes dip lower, over her flat stomach to her slender thighs and then down over pale

stockinged legs, before they made the same journey back
up her face again.

'Where are we?' she asked, using the cover of fastening
her jacket buttons.

'The island of Skiathos,' he told her. 'I have a villa here.
It will, of course, be sold when I get back the family island,' he added stiffly.

The family island... Mia shuddered, swallowing on the
thick dry lump that formed in her throat at the grim reminder of what this was all about for him.

Then he went on, in a completely different tone of voice,
'That green colour suits you,' he murmured huskily. 'It
does something spectacular to your eyes.'

She was so disconcerted by the unexpected compliment
that she just stared blankly at the mint green suit with its
little fitted jacket and short straight skirt. She hadn't bought
it for its colour, but out of respect for the icy winter weather
back in London. The suit was made from pure cashmere
with matching dyed fake fur collar and cuffs to the jacket.

'Thank you,' she replied, having to fight the rather pa-
thetic urge to blush because he had said something nice to
her.

A small silence fell, she wasn't sure why. The two of
them stood there, seemingly imprisoned by it, she with her
head lowered and he—well, she didn't know what he was
doing because she didn't dare look. But the sudden tension
between them was almost palpable. Then someone was
opening the outer door of the plane and, thankfully, the
strange tension was broken.

He left the aircraft first, obviously expecting her to follow. She did so reluctantly, to find another car was waiting
for them at the bottom of the short flight of steps—a silver
Mercedes.

The sun was shining and the air was much warmer than
it had been back in England, but not so hot that she didn't
appreciate the warm suit she was wearing.

Alexander was striding round to the driver's side of the car while their luggage was being stowed in the boot. Taking a deep breath, Mia stepped up to the passenger door and then, on a strange kind of compulsion, she paused to glance across the shimmering silver bonnet towards him.

And there it was—the first time that their eyes truly met. Her heart stopped, the breath squeezing painfully in her stilled lungs. He looked grim, those dark eyes frowning back at her with a resentment that utterly belied his earlier compliment.

He hated and despised her for bringing him down to this level. And, what was worse, she didn't even blame him. She hated and despised herself! So why should it hurt?

Yet it did. Of course it hurt. She had feelings, like anyone else! It was her eyes that dropped first, hiding the sudden sharp stab of pain she was experiencing—hiding the deep, dragging sense of self-loathing with which she was having to live.

Heart-weary, she made herself get into the car. He didn't join her immediately. In fact, he remained standing out there for such a long, long time that Mia began to wonder if he had finally come to his senses and changed his mind about all of this. Eventually he appeared, folding his long body into the seat beside her.

He didn't look at her again, and she didn't look at him. The car began to move, and the atmosphere inside it was so thick you could almost suffocate in it. 'It isn't too late to stop this if you want to,' she heard herself whisper, hoping... Hoping for what? she asked herself.

'No,' he replied.

Relief washed through her because that, she realised bleakly, was what she'd been hoping he'd say. No matter how much she hated this she still wanted it—needed it. Needed him.

Her new surroundings were lush and green, with bright splashes of colour from a flush of very early blooming flowers. Give it another few months and the green would be baked brown by the heat of the sun, she mused sadly. The flowers would be mostly gone. It was Mother Nature's way of maintaining a balance—hours of unrelenting sunshine but at the expense of floral colour.

Was she destined to wilt along with the flowers as the months went by? she wondered. She had the feeling that that was exactly what she would do, living a life in an emotion-starved desert with this man.

So, what's new? She mocked her own maudlin fancy. You've been living just like that with your own father. Swapping one heartless despot for another isn't going to be that much of a hardship, is it?

They were travelling along a high, winding road with the sea to the left of them. They passed through tiny hamlets of whitewashed buildings, which would probably be alive with tourists in high season but were at present almost deserted. There was hardly anyone about, in fact. It was a point she dared to remark upon to the man beside her.

'Most people here spend their winters on the mainland,' he explained. 'There is work for them there out of season, and the weather here can be as cold as England sometimes. But in another couple of months the place will come alive again.'

'Is it a big island?' she asked curiously.

He shook his dark head. 'We have driven almost its full length already,' he said. 'The house is situated in the next bay.'

Five minutes later they were driving through the gates of what appeared to be a vast private property hidden from the road by a high wall flanked by tall shrubs and trees. The house itself nestled lower down so the only view she got of it was its red slate rooftop.

It was impossible to tell just how big it was, but as they dropped lower she counted six separate windows on the upper floor and four on the lower, split by a wide white arched double door in the centre of a veranda.

By the time they came to a halt at the veranda steps she had counted at least four men who could only have been security guards by the way they made themselves evident as the car pulled in each one of them in turn, giving an acknowledging flick of his hand before he slunk out of sight again.

'Well, this is it,' Alexander announced, leaning back in his seat as the car engine died into silence. 'Your new home for the duration.'

Mia made no comment—what could she say? Oh, how lovely? How enchanting? I'm sure I will be happy here? She knew for a fact he had no interest in making her happy.

Anyway, she was too busy stifling the fresh set of butterflies that were attacking her system, apprehension for what was in store for her next being their stimulus.

She opened her door and made herself climb out into the late afternoon sunshine. Once again Alexander took his time to do the same, remaining seated inside the car as though it gave him a chance to relax his cold features and let them show what he was really feeling.

Anger, mostly, she guessed, a bitter sense of resentment at her presence in his life, which was going to be her close companion for what he had called the duration.

The white entrance doors began to open. Mia stood, watching, as they swung wide and a short stocky woman stepped out, dressed in uniform grey.

Her expression was utterly impassive as she studied Mia for a few short seconds, then turned her attention away as Alexander Doumas uncoiled himself from the car. Then a smile of such incredible warmth lit the woman's rugged features that it made the comparison between welcome and no welcome with a hard, cruel alacrity.

She said something in Greek, and he replied in the same language as he strode up the steps towards her. They did not embrace, which killed Mia's suspicion that this woman might be his mother. Then they were both turning to gaze in her direction, and all warmth left both of them. Mia's chin came up accordingly, pride insisting she outface the enemy to her last breath.

'Come.' That was all he said, as if he were talking to a pet dog.

Come. Sucking back the wretched desire to tell him to go to hell, she walked around the car and up the steps with her clear green gaze fixed defiantly somewhere between the two of them.

'This is Elena,' she was informed. 'She is my house-keeper here. Anything you require you refer to her. Elena will show you to your room,' he added coolly. 'And get Guido to bring up your luggage. I have some calls to make.'

And he was gone. Without a second look in Mia's direction, he strode into the house and disappeared.

'This way, madam...' Surprising Mia with her nearly accent-free English, the housekeeper turned and led the way into the house.

It was warmer inside, with sunlight seeping in through silk-draped windows onto apricot walls and lovingly polished wooden floors and doors. The furniture was old, undoubtedly antique, but solid, with a well used, well lived with look to it. Not what she would have expected of him somehow.

A highly polished wooden staircase climbed up the wall to the left of her, then swept right around the upper landing.

Elena led the way up and across the polished floor to a door directly opposite the stairs. She threw it open then stood back to allow Mia to move past her.

Her feet were suddenly sinking into a deep-piled oatmeal carpet, and her eyes drifted around soft lemon walls and white woodwork. Oatmeal curtains were caught back from the windows with thick lemon ropes.

'Your bathroom is to your right,' Elena informed her

coolly. 'The master's bedroom is through the door to your left.'

Separate bedrooms, then, Mia was relieved to note. 'Thank you,' she murmured, and forced herself to step further into the room.

Elena did not join her, instead remaining in the open doorway. 'My daughter, Sofia, will come and unpack for you. If you need anything tell her and she will tell me.'

In other words, don't speak to me yourself unless it is absolutely necessary, Mia ruefully assumed from that cold tone.

'Guido, my husband, will bring your luggage shortly,' the housekeeper continued. 'Dinner here is served at nine. Will you require some refreshment before then?'

And doesn't it just stick in your throat to offer it? Mia thought with a sudden blinding white smile that made the other woman's face drop at the sheer unexpectedness of it.

'Yes,' she said lightly. 'I require a large pot of coffee, milk—not cream—to go with it and a plate of sandwiches—salad, I think. Thank you, Elena. Now you may go.'

The woman's face turned beetroot red as she stepped back over the threshold, then pulled the door shut with a barely controlled click. Almost immediately Mia wilted, the stress of maintaining this level of indifference towards everyone taking the strength out of her legs so that she almost sank shakily into the nearest chair.

Right in the very midst of that telling little weakness she sucked in a deep breath, straightening her shoulders and grimly defying it. She had many long months of this to put up with, and if she started turning into a quivering wreck at each new obstacle she wouldn't stay the course.

With that now aching chin held high again, she turned to view the room in general. It was large and light and airy, with two full-length windows standing open to a light breeze beyond. Appropriate furniture stood around the room—a couple of oatmeal upholstered bedside chairs and a small matching sofa scattered with pale lemon cushions. A large dark wood wardrobe stood against the wall opposite the windows, a dressing-table against another, and a tall chest of drawers. Her eyes kept moving, picking out occasional tables and table lamps sitting on lace doilies to protect the polished wood—all very old-fashioned and reminiscent of a different era when tender loving care was poured into furniture like this in the form of beeswax, which she could smell in the air.

And then, of course, there was the bed.

Gritting her teeth, Mia made herself turn and face her major fear. The bed was huge, standing in pride of place between the two open windows, its heavily carved head- and footboards suggesting that the bed was antique. The sheets were white and folded back neatly over a pale lemon bedspread, the headboard piled with snowy white pillows.

Her heart stopped beating, her stomach muscles contracting with dread as she stood there staring at it. She made herself imprint the image of two heads on those snowy white pillows—one dark and contemptuous but grimly determined, the other red-gold and frightened but resolutely defiant.

She shuddered suddenly, realising that contempt and defiance were not going to make good bed partners. Contempt and mute submission would be a far less volatile mixture, she told herself in an attempt at wry mockery.

It didn't work. In fact, there wasn't even the merest hint of the usual mockery that she relied on so much to keep her going.

Oh, hell, she thought heavily, and moved around the bed to go and went to open one of the windows, her lungs pulling in short tugs of clean fresh air in an effort to dispel the ever-present sense of dread—a dread that was drawing nearer with every passing hour.

There was a pretty view outside, she noted in a deliberate

MICHELLE REID

grim thoughts. Carefully attended gar-
towards a shallow rock face, but she
...ach or any obvious way down the cliff to

...was a glass-walled swimming pool glinting off
...of her, which cheered her up a bit because at
...emperature was mild enough to allow her to take
...al exercise while she was stuck here. Further out,
...ould see the misted bulk of several other islands not
...y far away. It made her wish she'd had the foresight to
...where he was bringing her so she could have bought
...f a map and acquainted herself with what she was
...bout there.

S... another thought hit her, making a connection that
island he... have made ages ago. For this was Skiathos, and
...nged to the Sporades group of isl...
...er owned was al... also in the Sporades group.

...or islands. The
island her...nged ... also in the Sporades group.
She could actually be looking at her new husband's dream,
without actually knowing it.

Suddenly she felt surrounded by reminders of what she
was here for. The island. The bed. The isolation in which
she was supposed to fulfil her part of the bargain.

Her blood ran cold and she shivered, any pleasure she
had experienced because of the beauty of her new surroundings spoiled for ever. She turned away from the window,
from the islands, from the bed, and walked straight into the
bathroom.

She needed a shower, she decided grimly—needed to
soak the tension out of her body with warmth. She had to
keep herself together because this was the beginning, not
the end, of it.

Guido had arrived with her luggage while she was still
in the bathroom and Sofia was there when Mia eventually
came back to the bedroom, wrapped in a white terry bathrobe she had found hanging on the bathroom door and with
her hair hidden beneath a turban-wrapped towel.

THE PRICE OF A

Sofia's glance was very guarded

in badly broken English, 'and have un

'Thank you.' No smile was offered so

The girl left and Mia moved over to t

low table beside the sofa. The coffee was

the crusty bread sandwiching the salad too th

her to have any hope of swallowing it past that

was still constricting her throat. Luckily, someone

the foresight to place a pitcher of iced water on th

picked the salad off the bread.

with the coffee so she contented her thirst with that

By the time she had finished she felt suddenly and utterly

bone-weary. Despite her long shower, the strain of it

was still dragging at her muscles and she could

dull throb of a tension headache coming on

she at last did what her

her to do si

With a heavy sigh,
body had been pleading with her
here. She got up and walked over to that dreaded bed, threw herself face downwards across it and simply switched off.

For the next few blissful hours Mia was aware of nothing, not the day slowly closing in around her or the towel turban slowly uncoiling itself from her head then sliding lazily to the carpet—trailing her hair along with it so the long silken strands spilled over the edge of the bed like a wall of fire lit by the glowing sunset.

When she did eventually come awake she did so abruptly, not sure what had woken her but certain that something had. Her eyes flicked open, her senses coming to full alert and setting her flesh tingling.

She continued to lie there for a few more seconds, listening intently to the silence surrounding her, then something brushed against her cheek and on a strangled gasp she rolled over—and found herself wedged up against a hard male body that was reclining beside her. Alexander's dark head was casually propped up on the heel of one hand.

'I wondered how long your hair was,' he remarked idly. 'Now I know...'

It was then she realised that he was gently fondling a silky skein of her hair. Her scalp was tingling, as well as her cheek, as if he'd teasingly brushed the lock of hair across it.

It must have been his touch that had woken her. 'W-what are you doing here?' she demanded unsteadily.

Stupid question, his mocking eyes said, and he grinned, all white teeth and predatorial amusement.

With a flash of annoyance, meant to disguise the real shaft of alarm that went streaking through her, Mia made to roll away from him again but he stopped her, his arm snaking around her waist to keep her clamped against him.

She met with rock-solid immovable muscle and soft white terry towelling. Her breath caught her eyes dropping to stare at the gap in his bath-robe where tight black curls of rough chest hair lay clustered against warm golden skin.

Her heart stuttered. Her mouth went dry. Something clicked into motion deep inside her—the slowly turning gears of sexual awakening, she realized with dread.

'You sleep like an innocent, do you know that?' he informed her very softly. 'I've been lying here for ages, just watching you, and you barely moved, barely breathed, and your lovely mouth looked so vulnerable it was a strain not to kiss it.'

He did now, though, bending his dark head just enough to brush his lips against her own. Her own head jerked backwards in rejection. 'L-let go of me,' she stammered. 'I n-need—'

'Sex on demand,' he reminded her, speaking right over her protest. 'You agreed to it. Here I am to collect it.'

Oh, God. Her eyes closed, her lips folding in on themselves in an effort to moisten what had gone way beyond being moistened. 'Please,' she whispered with the first hint of weakness she had let herself show him. 'I'm not used to...'

'Performing on demand?' he suggested when her voice trailed off into silence. 'That's not the way I heard it...'

Silence. Mia went perfectly still, a slither of horror sliding down her spine. 'I don't know what you mean,' she said.

'No?' he murmured. 'Then, please, correct me if I am wrong,' he drawled. 'You did have your first full-blown affair at the tender age of sixteen, did you not? With a struggling rock star, I believe. He died several years later of a cocktail of drink and drugs. But not before your wild whoring ways forced your father to place you in a closed institution while they dried you out, made you a half-fit human being then disgorged you back on society in the hope that you had learned your lesson. Did you learn your lesson?'

Mia felt sick, but said nothing. Her father, she was thinking desolately, just couldn't let her do anything with a modicum of dignity. He had to soil it—soil everything—for her.

'Certainly,' that cruel voice went on when she offered no defence, 'you've kept a very low profile for the last seven years. Do you still indulge in drugs?'

She shook her head. Her eyes were closed, and her face so white it looked brittle. It would be no use telling him that she had never—ever—abused her body with illegal drugs because she knew he wouldn't believe her.

'I don't want any child of mine born a drug addict because his mother had no control over herself. What about sex?' he pushed on remorselessly. 'Should I have had you tested before we reached this point? Is there any chance I am likely to put my health at risk if I indulge myself with you?'

Her heart heaved, her aching lungs along with it. 'I have not had a sexual relationship with a man in years,' she told him with as much pride as she could muster.

'You expect me to believe that?'

'It's the truth,' she retorted, her green eyes despising him so much that they actually sought glacial contact with his. 'Believe it or not. I don't care. I don't care if you get a whole army of doctors in here to make sure I am clean enough for you to use. But just do it quickly, will you, so we can get the whole sordid conception over with?'

With that, she managed to break free from him and rolled sideways across the bed. His hand shot out and caught her.

'Oh, no, you don't,' he breathed, and began to pull her to him.

He came to lean right over her, his face tight with anger, his eyes alive with it and his body tense with it. 'Is it true?' he demanded rawly. 'Is everything I've just said the truth?'

The truth? she repeated to herself with skin-blistering mockery. He would like the truth even less than he was liking her father's lies!

'I sold myself for five million pounds,' she spat. 'Does that answer your question?'

It had been a reckless thing to say—foolish, when it was so obvious that he was angry. His dark eyes flashed contemptuously. 'Then start paying your damned dues,' he muttered, and his mouth crushed hers.

It was an insult, an invasion. It promised nothing but punishment for believing she could answer him like that. Yet what actually happened to her then was perhaps more of a punishment than the fierceness of his kiss.

Because she pushed and punched out at him—and then went up like an exploding volcano, her mouth drawing greedily on his like someone with a raging thirst. It was awful—she could feel herself shattering into a million fiery particles but couldn't do a single thing to stop it from happening.

'My God,' he gasped, dragging his mouth free so he could stare down at her. He was shocked. She didn't blame him—she was feeling utterly shattered by it herself!

'You are now contaminated!' she snarled at him in sheer seething reaction.

He just laughed, but it was a rather shocked sound with nothing amused about it. Then he caught her mouth again, sending her spinning back to where she'd gone off to with no apparent effort. It was different now. There was no anger feeding the flames, just a white-hot passion that sang through her blood and sizzled across her skin.

His hands were all over her, his long fingers knotting in her hair, trailing the arching length of her throat, urgently searching for and finding the thrusting tightness of her breast. Then, frustratingly, his hands moving on downwards, finding the knot holding her robe together and impatiently freeing it.

Cool fresh air touched her burning skin and she cried out when it actually hurt. His mouth had left hers and she hadn't even noticed, his body sliding sideways so he could completely unwrap her.

Her eyes were closed, her body trembling with an overload of sensation. He knelt there beside her and watched it all happen while he rid himself of his own robe, his dark face taut and muscles bunched, his own sensual urgency no less controlled than hers was.

When he came back to her, her arms wrapped round him, her fingers clawing into his hair. Their mouths fused hungrily again, and she felt the stinging pleasure of his hair-roughened chest grazing the sensitised tips of her breasts. She felt the power of his arousal pressing against her thighs and instinctively opened them so she could accept him into the cradle of her slender hips.

He groaned something, she didn't know what. She didn't even care. But her eyes snapped open in protest when he denied her his mouth again.

He was glaring hotly down at her. 'Wild,' he muttered. 'I knew you would be wild. No one with this glorious colour of hair and the amount of self-control you exhibit could be anything but wild once you let go.'

'I haven't let go!' she denied, wishing it was the truth! 'I hate you!' she added helplessly

'I hate you too.' He laughed. 'Interesting, isn't it? How two people who can hate each other this much can also feel this naked kind of passion.'

'The passion is all yours,' she said, tight-lipped, then gasped when he suddenly lifted himself away from her to kneel between her parted thighs.

Eyes like black lasers skimmed over her body from firm proud, thrusting breasts to the cluster of tight golden curls protecting her sex.

'Oh...' she choked in appalled embarrassment. No man had ever looked on her quite like this!

But what was a worse humiliation was the way her senses were responding to the way he was looking at her— throbbing and pulsing with an excitement that threatened to completely engulf her.

'I can see you are dying for me to touch you.'

'Please,' she groaned in pained mortification. 'Don't do this to me!'

'You will be wishing me inside you before this hour is through,' he promised darkly.

Then he touched her, sliding a long and silkenly practi- sed finger along the hot moist crevice he had exposed with such a bold disregard to her modesty, and claimed posses- sion by delving deep inside.

It shook her, shook her right through to the very centre of everything she had ever imagined to do with this kind of intimacy. At sixteen she had been too young and too inexperienced to know that she was supposed to have been enjoying this as much as the man who had eventually taken her virginity.

But this—this wild hot surge of stinging pleasure which was taking her over was completely new territory to her. And the fact that it was caused by a man she so utterly despised was enough to send her reeling into shock—the kind of shock that held her helpless as he arched his body over her, capturing her mouth with a hunger that devoured while his fingers began to work a magic on her flesh she had never experienced in her life before.

Oh, help me, she thought on a wave of helpless despair. She couldn't believe this was happening to her, couldn't believe she could lose control like this!

He knew it too, and played with her, like a cat with a mesmerised mouse. An arm slid beneath her shoulders, his body shifting sideways so he was no longer completely covering her, then the real torture began, with slow, light, lazy caresses that told him everything he needed to know about the woman he was exploring.

He touched her face, her nose, her lips, and ran those same fingers down her neck and between the throbbing upthrust of her breasts. He followed the flat line of her ribcage to her tightly muscled stomach, traced the line of her hips, then delved once again into the very core of her, but only fleetingly—too fleetingly—before he was exploring her silken thighs, watching with a dark intensity, which really frightened her, each quiver and jolt of her flesh as he learned what gave her pleasure and what did not.

'Why do you always hide your hair?' he murmured huskily into the dark chasm of sensation that her whirling mind had become. 'I find it very exciting that the same colour nestles here between your thighs. I adore it that your skin is so pale against my own skin, that your breasts are so very sensitive to my slightest touch even though you fight me. And even the fact that you fight me excites me. It makes me wonder what I will feel when you decide to torment me in return...'

'No.' Out of her head with sensation as she was, she heard the silky invitation in his voice and breathlessly refused the offer. 'I won't touch you. You don't need me to.'

The obvious fact that his manhood lay in such daunting erection against her thigh confirmed that fact.

'I will drive you wild,' he warned her, seeming even to enjoy this battle. As if any battle with her was an excitement for him. 'I will make you beg...'

Mia kept her hands clenched in tight fists by her sides as a stubborn answer.

She heard his soft laugh at her stubbornness, then he took one pointed stinging nipple into his mouth and sucked hard at the same time as he slid a finger deep inside her.

Wild, he'd called her. Well, she went wild. It flared up with no constraint. Her hands snaked up and caught at his hair, her fingernails raking into his scalp as she cried out in a wretchedly raw response to what he was doing to her.

He muttered something—it sounded shaken. Then he was repeating the sequence of events so that she reacted in the same way. It was so utterly, mind-blowingly pleasurable that she didn't even feel ashamed of herself, just elated— so exquisitely elated because she had truly believed that she did not have it in her to respond to any man as violently as this.

'You will beg me or caress me,' he warned.

Her eyes flicked open, green fire lasering into burning black. 'I never beg,' she informed him with amazing coolness.

'No?'

With a sudden bright glow in his eyes he slid down the full length of her, landing on his knees beside the bed. 'Beg?' he offered silkily.

'Go to hell, Mr Doumas,' she bit out, using that formal title as an insult.

What he did was bury his mouth between her thighs.

Mia begged. She clutched at him in exquisite agony, and pleaded with him to stop. She wrapped her long legs around him and tried to pull him up and over her. She dug long anxious fingers into his sweat-slicked shoulders. She gasped and writhed and panted and hated him with a vengeance as he held her fast with hands at her hips and drove her to the very edge of sanity.

'Oh—please,' she sobbed, 'please stop now!'

'Say my name,' he muttered against her flesh, his tongue making a snake-like flick at her with the cruel intention of ripping the breath from her body. 'Beg me again and use my name.'

'Alexander,' she whispered helplessly.

'Alex,' he corrected. 'My lovers call me Alex.'

'Alex!' she groaned. 'Alex, please, please...' she murmured deliriously.

'Please—what?' he demanded.

'Please come inside me!' she cried out in aching agony.

It was so humiliating because he laughed as he slid his long, lean, hot body along the full length of her, then entered her with no more warning than that.

'Like this?' he taunted. 'Is this what the five-million-pound wife requires?'

But it was too late for Mia. The cruelty and the insult went sailing right past her because she had shot straight into an orgasm that went on and on and on, and made him go very still in stunned reaction.

He could feel her—actually feel her beating all around him on wave after wave of pulsing ecstasy. It shook him, shook to the very roots his conviction that he'd often experienced what was best in a sexual climax. This woman was experiencing what had to be the best, and not one part of her missed out on the raging feast. Not her fingers where they flexed and clutched at his body, not her breasts as they heaved and arched and quivered, not her mouth as it gasped and groaned and panted.

He caught her mouth. He needed to capture it, needed to join in that wild experience, and at last he began to move inside her, feeling that incredible orgasm go on and on and on while driving him towards his own mind-blowing finish.

When it came he lost touch with himself, with her, with everything. His mind shut down. He felt it happen—felt the flow of blood leave his brain as it surged down to that point of such unbelievable pleasure that it was almost agony to feel it eventually fade away.

Mia thought she might have died a little afterwards. Certainly something deep inside her had been lost for ever. She didn't know what, couldn't begin to try and work out what. But as he lay there, heavy on her, his big body still attacked by the pulsing aftershocks of what they had just created between them, she knew that something vital had gone from her—had been passed, maybe, from her to him, she didn't know.

But it was most definitely gone.

When he eventually moved, sliding sideways onto the mattress to bury his face in the pillow, Mia turned and curled up away from him. She was shocked, shocked by the uninhibited wildness of what had just taken place. Shocked by the power of his passion and her own ability to let go of every ounce of self-control.

And now came the aftermath, she thought bleakly as they continued to lie there, together but separate, intimate but strangers.

Silent, appalled strangers who had been caught in the tangled web of their own sexuality, only to find after it all that they were still very separate entities.

He moved first, sending her muscles into wary tension as he moved to the edge of the bed and sat up with his feet on the floor. She heard him utter a heavy sigh, sensed him raking angry fingers through hair that had been disarrayed by her own restless fingers. She felt the mattress dip as he bent and she knew he was picking up his discarded robe. She felt him begin to cover himself as he pushed himself to his feet.

Tears burned in her eyes as she lay there, facing away from him with her arms and hands clutched protectively across her curved and naked body. She sensed his eyes raking over her, sensed him considering what to say, and waited with baited breath and a hammering heart for the clever insult to hit her eardrums.

But in the end he said nothing, and maybe that was just about the biggest insult he could have paid her as he walked out of her bedroom in total silence.

CHAPTER FOUR

IT TOOK every ounce of determination Mia could muster to step out of that bedroom at precisely nine o'clock that evening, but she had to pause at the top of those highly polished stairs as a bout of cowardly tremors made a sudden last-minute attack.

She was still suffering from shock, she knew. Her body was in shock at the unrestrained way it had behaved this afternoon. Her mind was in shock because it just could not believe it had allowed her to go so out of control with Alex, a man she supposedly felt nothing for. But, more to the point, she was finding it more difficult to come to terms with the knowledge that she had allowed all of it to happen with a man who felt so little for her.

Where had her pride been? Her self-respect?

She didn't know, could not understand what had possessed her during that wild, hot frenzy that had taken place in the bedroom. But she certainly knew where her pride was at this moment. It was floundering around at her feet, along with her lost self-respect.

And the urge to simply turn right around and lock herself in that bedroom rather than have to face *him* again tonight was so powerful at the moment that she almost gave in to it.

Then the sound of a door opening downstairs caught her attention, and she suddenly discovered that her pride was not completely demolished because, with a bracing of her slender shoulders and a defiant lifting of her chin, she found herself walking down the stairs, instead of dashing for cover behind a locked door, because she knew she would rather die than let him see how utterly degraded she felt.

A sound to her left as she reached the hallway set her feet moving in that direction. A door was standing slightly ajar, with golden light shining gently through the gap.

She took a deep breath, ran trembling fingers down her equally trembling thighs then stepped forward, silently pushing the door open just enough to allow her to enter whatever room was on the other side of it.

She saw Alex immediately. Her heart turned over, her throat locking on a fresh lump of tension. He was dressed very formally in a black silk dinner suit, white dress shirt and black bow tie—though what he was wearing barely registered with her at that moment because she was so busy coming to terms with the way she was seeing him now.

Naked.

She shuddered, horrified at herself—appalled by the sudden flare of sexual awareness that went sizzling through her as her eyes looked at him and saw firm golden flesh, covering a beautifully structured framework, instead of the reality of conventional black fabric.

She saw wide satin-smooth shoulders and rock-solid biceps, a hair-roughened chest that was so powerfully muscled it made her own breasts sting in memory of what it had felt like to be crushed against it. She saw a long lean torso with a tight waist, flat hips and strong thighs, supporting a pelvis that housed the full-blooded and dynamic essence of the man.

An essence that made her inner thighs clench, made her go hot all over, made her lungs completely shut down as a whole gamut of sensation went racing right through her. She looked at his mouth and felt it crushing her own mouth, looked at his hands and felt them caressing her skin.

She looked at the man in his entirety and saw a tall dark stranger—now an intimate stranger. But one who had suddenly become so physically real to her that she now realised just how successfully she had been blanking him out before as a flesh and blood person.

Was he aware she had done that? she wondered as she stood there, staring at him in nerve-tightening tension. Did he know that to get herself this far in this dastardly deal they had struck she'd had to pretend he was nothing more than a shadow?

Standing there by a drinks cabinet, seemingly lost in thought as he frowned into what looked like a crystal tumbler lightly splashed with whisky, the only thing she could be sure about concerning him now was that at this moment, while he believed himself alone, he was doing nothing to hide his own sense of loathing at what had erupted between them.

And why not? she asked herself. He despised her as much as she despised him so it followed automatically that he felt the same revulsion for what they'd done to each other.

Shame trickled through her, followed by a wave of pained helplessness. Because this was only the beginning, not the end.

The beginning.

She must have moved, though she hadn't been aware of doing it, because something made his dark head turn. Then he became still, his brooding stare fixing on hers, knowledge making his dark brown irises glint and then burn, which sent a wild flush of hot embarrassment sweeping through her because their new intimacy, she realised, was catching him out, too.

Then the flame changed to contempt, a hard, biting, cruel contempt, before he hooded the expression with long black lashes. Hooded it so he could let his gaze run over her carefully controlled hair and the dramatically plain deep turquoise silk shift dress she was wearing, which skimmed her slender figure without clinging anywhere—deliberately chosen for that reason.

Yet he missed nothing—like herself, she suspected, seeing not the fully dressed woman standing here but the naked one, the wild one, the woman who had surprised him with the power of her own passions. He was seeing her spread out, fully exposed to him and ready.

She felt sick suddenly. Stomach-churningly, head-swimmingly sick.

'Take your hair out of that unflattering knot,' he said in an oddly flattened tone. 'And don't wear it up in my company again.'

It was a shock. The very last thing she had expected him to say, in fact. Her hair? An impulsive hand went to touch the simple knot held in place by a tortoiseshell clasp. Her cheeks warmed and her eyes dropped away from him because she didn't know why he was suddenly attacking her and why he had used that strange tone to do it.

'No,' she said, grimly pulling herself together, the coolly indifferent Mia sliding back into place. 'It's more comfortable for me to wear it like this. It annoys me when it's loose.'

'Then suffer,' he said unsympathetically. 'I hate liars. And that prim hairstyle makes such a damned liar of you. At least when your hair is down...' he took a tense gulp at the drink in his glass '...people are forewarned about what you really are.'

'And what am I?' she asked, the green eyes glinting with challenge—while every fine muscle in her body was held tensely, waiting for him to say the word her father had been throwing at her for so many years now that she couldn't remember when he had not seen her as a whore.

This man would be no different. This man and her father had so much in common it would shock and appal Alexander Doumas to know just how much.

Or maybe he did know, she corrected herself when he didn't say it but took another deep slug from his glass instead.

'Do it,' he commanded as he lowered the glass again. 'Or I will make you do it.'

'Dinner,' a carefully neutral voice announced behind Mia.

She turned abruptly and caught Elena's frosty expression. She knew the other woman had overheard most of their telling little conversation, and looked right through the housekeeper as she strode proudly past her.

But the hand landing on her shoulder brought her to a sudden standstill. How Alex had managed to move across the room so quickly Mia didn't know, but it was certainly his hand, burning its already familiar brand as he detained her.

'Leave us.' He grimly dismissed the housekeeper.

She turned and left as he propelled Mia back into the room then closed the door. A half-moment later and the tortoiseshell clasp that was holding up her hair was springing free, and the silken coil of hair was unfurling over his fingers in a heavy fall of fire that rippled its way to the base of her spine.

The tortoiseshell clasp was discarded and she heard it land with a clunk on a nearby table. Then he turned her round to face him.

'Don't fight me,' he warned her very grimly, 'because you won't like the consequences.'

To prove his point, the hand still lost in her hair tightened, tugging her head backwards until she had no choice but to look at him. His eyes were still hooded, but she could see the anger simmering beneath those heavy eyelids as he began to rearrange her hair to his own satisfaction.

It hurt her inside. For some reason Mia could not work out at all the way he was asserting his control over her like this hurt—when it shouldn't. It was only what she had expected from him from the very beginning after all.

'You don't like who you are, do you?' he murmured suddenly.

'No,' she replied. It was blunt and it was honest.

'It is why you hide your true nature behind prim clothes and stark hairstyles. You are ashamed of what you are.'

'Yes,' she confirmed, again with the same cool bluntness.

'But you could not keep the passion hidden in that bed upstairs, could you? It broke free and virtually consumed you.'

'You weren't so controlled yourself,' she hit back.

'I didn't quite reach the point where I completely stopped breathing,' he countered grimly.

Her cheeks went pale, her lowered eyes squeezing together on a fresh bout of self-revulsion.

'Was it like that with the rock star?' he questioned. 'Did you fall apart as spectacularly for him as you did for me?'

She didn't answer that one—refused to answer. Whatever had gone on in her life *before* this man was none of his business, and she was damned if she was going to feed his ego by telling him she had *never* lost control of herself like that before—ever.

His hand came to her chin, closed around it then tightened, demanding an answer, but her eyes showed him nothing except cold, green defiance. Her mouth, so red and full and still clearly swollen from his kisses, remaining resolutely shut.

'Well, I tell you this much, *yineka mou*,' he murmured very softly. 'You have set your own boundaries with what took place up there. You will not move from this estate without my say-so. You will not be left alone—either in this house of out of it—with another man. You are now, in effect, my personal prisoner.'

'Points you had written into my contract,' she reminded him. 'Did you see me arguing with you about them then?'

'Ah, but I have a... worrying suspicion that you were not so aware of your own passions when you agreed to that contract. Now you do know, and I am going to take no chances with you falling apart like that for any other man—understand me?'

'Yes.' Once more she refused to give him the satisfaction of arguing the point with him because, whatever lessons he thought he had learned about her in that blasted bedroom, she, too, had learned her own lessons about him. This man thrived on argument. His sexual drive fed off it, but he would not be fed by her again.

He knew exactly what she was doing, of course. He was not an idiot. He could read silent messages just as well as she could. But to her surprise, he laughed, a warm, dark, sexily amused sound that curled up her toes inside her shoes as his mouth came down to cover her own.

Their bodies fused, that quickly and that easily, from mouth to breast to hips. They came together as though someone or something had simply thrown a switch to let the whole wretched current of electric pleasure wrap itself around them.

His tongue blended with hers, and her hands jerked up to clutch at his warm, tightly muscled neck where her fingers spread along his jawbone, his cheeks and the smooth line of his chin. She felt his body respond by tensing, felt his hands drag their way downwards until they were clasping her low on the hips, drawing her even closer to the pulsing throb where his manhood was thickening, tightening.

Her own body melted—melted on the inside, melted on the outside, a hot, honeyed meltdown that poured into her bloodstream, filling her breasts and that aching junction between her thighs so she moved wantonly against him. She couldn't stop herself, couldn't put a halt to what was beginning to happen all over again.

She groaned—at least she thought it was her but it might have been him—and her thighs flexed and parted, searching out an even deeper intimacy against the grinding thrust of him. It was terrible. She didn't know herself, couldn't seem to control what was suddenly raging through her system.

When he dragged his mouth free she whimpered and

went in blind search of reconnection while his hands bit like twin vices into the flesh around her hips to keep her pressed tightly against him, though he denied her his mouth. Denied it ruthlessly. So much so that her eyes flickered open, glazed by need and a confusion that went so deep that it took several long agonising seconds for her to realise what he was doing.

Watching her.

Watching her with a bite in his eyes that told her exactly what he thought of her lack of control.

Whore, that expression said. Whore.

She almost fainted on the wave of self-loathing that went sweeping through her.

He despised her for responding like this—as much as he despised her for being here at all.

'Save it,' he said insolently, 'until later. I have a mistress to console before I can come back here and console you.'

It was cruel but, then, he had meant to be. Anger was driving him—anger at himself for wanting her like this, anger at her for making him want her and anger at the whole situation which he could only relieve by venting it on her.

With that final humiliation biting deep into her senses, he let go and stepped back from her. Two seconds after that he was pulling open the door and striding from the room. Not just from the room but from the villa. Standing there, trembling, aching and shamed, she listened to the front door slam in his wake, heard a car start up and drive away with a powerful roar.

And through it all she barely breathed, barely blinked, barely functioned on any level.

Why? Because it had finally sunk in just how much he hated her. It didn't matter that he had already told her so as far back as in her father's study—the point was that she hadn't really taken the full thrust of his words on board.

Words like, 'I will hate and despise you and bed you

with alacrity,' were suddenly taking on their full true meaning. As did his most recent statement, 'I have a mistress to console before I can come back here and console you...'

She would come second. Second to that lucky lady who probably came fairly far down his list of priorities, which made second a very low status indeed.

She was here for one purpose and one purpose only—to conceive his child so he could claim his prize.

'Your dinner, madam...' Sofia appeared from nowhere, her eyes lowered, her expression carefully guarded. 'The dining room is this way,' she prompted quietly.

It took another few moments to pull herself together but Mia managed it, following Sofia into the long narrow grandeur of a formal dining room where only one place setting waited.

He had always meant to leave her alone like this, she realised on a fresh wave of agony.

Then, thankfully, right out of the centre of that very same agony emerged the other Mia—the pragmatic, invulnerable, very mocking Mia. The one who could smile wryly at herself for actually being hurt by Alex's treatment of her.

The one who could sit quite comfortably at a table and eat alone because eating alone was far more preferable to eating with cruel swines like Alexander Doumas—a man like her father.

When the long silent meal was over she left alone, walking out of the dining room with her chin held high as she trod those polished stairs back to the relative sanctuary of her own room where she calmly prepared for bed—and felt the protective casing she had built around herself threaten to crack only once.

That was when she glanced at the bed she had so carefully tidied, before leaving the room earlier. Someone had stripped it, changed the sheets and put on a clean lemon top cover, one which gave not a single hint of what had taken place on that bed earlier—no tell-tale creases, nothing. An act which told tales in itself.

They knew.

She shuddered. The whole damned staff must know what had been going on in this bed earlier.

Did that mean they also knew why it had been going on? By their cold unwelcoming attitude she had to assume that they knew *exactly* why she was here and, worse, that their employer was accepting the situation only under the severest duress.

That brought her swiftly on to the next soul-crushing point—did they therefore know just where he had gone tonight?

The mistress.

The other woman.

Did they know that he had climbed out of her bed only to climb into another bed with his mistress?

Humiliation poured into her blood, searing a path to a temper few knew she possessed. With a flash from her glinting green eyes, she reached down and grabbed hold of that lemon cover, yanking it clear away from the bed and tossing it in a heap on the ground at her feet.

From now on, she vowed, every time she walked into this room she would mess up this rotten bed! If they wanted to bear witness to their employer's bed duty, let them! Let them change this damned bed fifteen times a day and wonder at his incredible stamina!

Keeping two women busy at the same time—the rotten, crass bastard!

Not that she cared! she told herself tightly as she crawled between those pristine white sheets. She couldn't give a damn what the man got up to so long as he was practising safe sex with the other woman. Other than that, she had no interest whatsoever in his sex life!

That was the exact point at which she made her brain switch off because she had a horrible feeling that she might begin to care if she let herself dwell on the subject too much.

Thankfully, sleep came to her rescue with a single lowering of her eyelids. Wearing a nightdress of cream satin and curled on her side with her long hair flowing across the white pillow, she didn't know another thing for hours. Hours and hours of blessed oblivion from the bleak prospect of what her life was going to be like from now on.

A hand grasped her shoulder. 'Wake up,' a deeply masculine voice insisted.

Just as she had managed to push it all away with the single blink of an eye, it was suddenly all back again. 'W-what?' she mumbled in sleepy confusion. 'What do you think you're doing!' she gasped as he rolled her onto her back and pinned her there with his weight. 'No—!'

'Not a word I recognise,' he informed her with a grim kind of sardonicism.

Her lashes flicked upwards, her eyes finding themselves trapped by glinting dark irises that confirmed exactly what his words and actions were stating.

'What's the matter?' she taunted. 'Wasn't she very consolable tonight?'

He frowned, his eyes narrowing for the few moments it took him to grasp her meaning. Then his teeth were suddenly gleaming in the darkness, cruel and incisive like the next few words he lashed her with. 'She was fine,' he muttered, 'but now I want you.'

'You're disgusting,' she said, and tried to wriggle free, but he wasn't about to let her.

'Nevertheless, when I want I take and you deliver,' he said harshly. 'Don't ever say no to me again.'

Then he did take, passionately and ruthlessly, his hungry mouth covering hers, his tongue probing with a dark, knowing intimacy that appalled her even as her own desires leapt like the traitors they were to greet him eagerly.

He still smelled of whisky. His lips were warm with it,

his tongue tasted of it, transferring the evocative taste to
her own tongue and filling her lungs with its heady fumes.
His hands were trembling slightly as though his urgency
was so great he was having difficulty controlling it. His
long fingers ran over the smooth slide of satin, skimming
her breasts, her ribcage, her abdomen and eliciting sharp
little stinging responses that made her gasp, her spine arch,
her muscles tighten and her hands move upwards to clutch
at his shoulders with the intention of pushing him away.

Only her hands never pushed. They made contact with
his hard, warm, naked flesh and clung to him, a wretched
groan escaping her smothered mouth as his fingers slid upwards to find her breasts again. In seconds her nipples were
erect and tingling, his palms rolling them with an erotic
expertise that had them pushing against the confines of her
nightdress while his thighs were insinuating themselves between her own.

The throbbing contact of his own powerful erection moving against fine satin was so intensely arousing that her
thighs widened even more in an effort to gain greater friction where she most needed it.

His mouth left hers and he laughed. It was a sound far
distant from humour but held angry triumph. 'What a hot
little thing you are when you let yourself go,' he taunted.
'No wonder you preferred me to that grotesque little man
who was knocking sixty. He could not have given you half
this much pleasure.'

'Your mind is a sewer,' she shot at him.

'My mind is that low?' he mocked, and grabbed hold of
the edge of her nightdress, tugged it up around her hips
and entered her. No foreplay, no compunction.

To her utter horror, Mia went wild beneath him. Just like
the last time, she was overtaken by an instant orgasm that
set her body writhing and her insides throbbing, the tiny
muscles inside rippling over him and around him as her

head fell back and her throat began to pant out little gasps of riotous intensity while her heart raced out of control.

It shocked him again, held him paralysed for the few stunning moments it took for him to accept just how spectacularly she responded to him. Then his mouth lowered to one tightly stinging nipple. Through the stretched tautness of her nightdress he sucked the pulsing tip deep into his mouth and began to move, thrusting his hips with short blunt stabs that kept her locked in that muscle-clenched storm of hectic climax, the strokes growing longer and deeper and harder as he drove her on and on with no let-up, no chance to make a mad grab at sanity.

She was out of her head and it dismayed her, but she couldn't seem to do a single thing about it. When he withdrew she should really have come tumbling back down to earth with a crash—but she didn't. She stayed up there, lost in that world of electric sensation.

He muttered something, which she couldn't make out. His body slid sideways, the nightgown coming off altogether before his mouth clamped on hers again and his fingers began to discover what his throbbing manhood already knew—what it was like to feel a woman in the throes of a multi-orgasm.

Those tormenting fingers stroked and incited her, his hungry tongue mimicking the action. One of her hands found his nape and clutched at it desperately, holding his mouth down on hers while her other hand went in agitated search of other parts of him.

He was so big, so hard and slick and potent—she wanted him back inside her. She wanted his mouth on her breasts but she wanted him to keep on kissing her mouth like this. In the end and on an impatient sigh her fingers clutched at a handful of his hair to tug his mouth from her so she could present him with her breast instead, and through it all her body was still rocketing through space on its own agenda.

He began to throb against her caressing hand. She felt it

happen and released a sigh of satisfaction that came out
closer to a salacious growl. She snaked her body beneath
him and guided him into her, two hands clutching at his
lean, tight buttocks.

Holding him like that, with his dark head buried between
her breasts, she let go of everything, driving him onward
with the thrust of her hips. Her cries of anguished pleasure
echoed around the darkened bedroom as she felt his own
pending climax build, felt the muscles bunch all over him,
heard his soft curse as his self-control began to crack wide
open, and this time they leapt together, high—so high Mia
felt lost and disembodied.

The next morning when she awoke the only sign that Alex
had ever been there was his scent on the sheets and on her
body—in her mouth and in the soft subtle pulse of her body
where he had so effectively stamped his presence.

It was a struggle to make herself get up. She almost
stumbled her way into the bathroom, felt hardly any better
by the time she came out again, and began to fumble round
for something to wear.

It was sunny outside, the heat of the day surprisingly
strong for this time of year, she discovered when she
pushed open the window in an effort to drag some air into
her lungs that did not smell of him.

It didn't work. He was in her system, she knew. Knew
the man and his scent were destined to be an innate part of
her for ever now.

It was a wretched thought—the kind of thought that
made her shiver, as if someone had just walked over her
grave, because she knew that no matter how passionately
she had affected him last night he would be despising her
more for the way she'd responded than he would have done
if she'd simply remained cold beneath him.

Oh, face it, Mia, she told herself grimly. You would be
despising yourself less if you'd managed to stay aloof—

and that's what is really troubling you. You're disgusted with yourself for being so sexually vulnerable to a man you hold so little respect for.

And, for all you know about him, he probably has the same effect on every woman he takes to his bed.

The great lover, she mocked acidly. The Don Juan of the nineteen-nineties!

Did that mean his mistress was well used to losing her head whenever he deigned to bed her?

Did it matter? she asked herself angrily as a nasty poison called jealousy began to creep through her blood. The point is, you respond like that and it's shameful!

But it didn't alter the fact that she fell apart in his arms like that every night for the next fortnight. During the day she didn't see him. He was never lying beside her when she woke in the morning. She got used to hearing a helicopter arrive and take off again very early—taking him to his offices in Athens, she presumed, though she was never given the opportunity to ask. He came back by the same means, usually just as dusk was beginning to colour the sky.

Where he ate she did not know, but it was never with her. The only contact they ever had was in the hours of darkness when he would slide into bed beside her and drive them both out of their heads with the devastating power of their mutual sensuality. He never spoke unless it was to comment on what they were doing, and he showed no remorse in using her like the brood mare she had sold herself as to him.

When it was over he would lie on his back beside her and she would curl on her side as far away from him as she could get while she waited for the aftershocks to stop shaking her body. Aftershocks she knew he was keenly aware of, and she had a feeling that they were the reason he lingered in that bed with her afterwards—because he saw those tremors as part of his due. They fed his ego—

an ego she knew had been badly damaged by him giving in to this deal in the first place.

Perhaps he even hated himself a little for giving in to it. Certainly, sometimes in the darkness she had glimpsed a look in his eyes that had suggested self-contempt as he'd watched her go wild beneath him and had known—just as she had—that he'd been about to join her.

Whatever he did to her, she did to him. If he did acquire that depth of pleasure with every woman he bedded, then he did not like it happening with her.

But, then, neither did Mia like it. In fact, towards the end of that first fortnight she began hoping—praying—that Mother Nature would be kind to her and make her pregnant. If the potency of their intercourse had anything to do with it, she should be very pregnant. Then at least he would leave her alone.

But it was not to be. The morning she woke with those familiar symptoms that warned her period had arrived she wept.

That day Mia roamed about the big empty house in a sluggish state of deep depression. It didn't help that there was not a friendly face in the place from whom she could gain some light relief from her own sense of grim failure.

Now she had to find a moment to break the unfortunate news to Alex that he had not succeeded in his quest to make her pregnant and, more to the point, that her body was not available to him for the next five days.

But how did she tell anything to a man who only came to her in the dead of night? Leave a note, pinned to the door between his bedroom and hers? she mused bitterly.

The temptation to do just that was so strong that she almost gave in to it. In the end she did the only thing she really could do, and waited up for him to come to her. When eventually she heard the connecting door open she was standing by the window, covered from neck to toe in soft white towelling.

She turned to face him. 'I'm not pregnant,' she announced boldly, and watched him stop dead in his tracks.

He didn't move again for the space of thirty long seconds, his stance so taut that she gained the rather satisfying impression that she had disconcerted him so much that he just did not know what to do next.

It was wonderful, almost worth the disappointment to see him so utterly stumped like this. He was a big man, a man whose body she knew so well by now that she could even read the frustration in his beautiful muscle formation.

'I suggest you use your mistress for the next few days,' she added with icy relish. 'I will, of course, let you know when I am available again.'

Oh, she enjoyed saying that! He treated her like a whore and she was responding as a whore. His dark lashes fluttered, folding down over his eyes then back up again as the full brutal smack of her words hit him full in his arrogant face.

Because he was no fool he recognised that she was not only acknowledging herself as a whore but that he was no better in his treatment of her.

But he got his own back. Heavens, did he get his own back! 'Fine,' he agreed smoothly. 'I will do that.'

The door closed behind him, leaving her standing there where she had faced up to him with her chin high and her stance proud, while the tears trickled unchecked down her pale cheeks.

Why was she crying? She didn't know. What had she expected, after all? For him to show disappointment, concern for her health, a bit of human compassion for her lonely plight?

The man didn't give a damn about her as a living, breathing human being, and went on to prove it by not coming back to the island for the next seven days.

A week to the day later, she was just climbing out of the swimming pool when Sofia came out onto the terrace. 'The master wishes to speak to you on the telephone,' she informed her.

The *master*. Mia mocked the title acidly. The man with everything—*master* of all he surveyed! Except an island he coveted and a child he hadn't managed to conceive.

'Thank you.' She nodded coolly to Sofia, grabbed her beach robe and pulled it over her dripping body as she followed the maid into the house and to a telephone extension in the drawing room.

'A helicopter is on its way to you,' Alex announced. 'It will arrive in about thirty minutes. It has no time to linger so be ready to board as soon as it lands.'

'But—'

That was as far as she got for the line went dead. Frowning slightly and wondering what this new development could mean because she had not been out of the confines of the estate since she'd arrived, she hurried upstairs, showered, dried her hair, then quickly knotted the still slightly damp mass at her nape. She threw on a pale blue cotton sundress, added a white linen jacket and gathered a few things together in a large white linen beach bag because she didn't know if she was going to be away for an hour or two or for a week.

She was waiting when the helicopter touched down on the purpose-built pad situated a little way off from one side of the house. The pilot didn't stop the rotors while he waited for her to duck beneath them and climb on board.

An hour later she was being transported by a chauffeur-driven limousine into the centre of Athens.

The car drew to a stop outside a residential apartment block, the driver getting out to escort her inside. He led her to the lift, smiled politely but briefly as he pressed a button on the lift console then stepped back again, leaving her to travel upwards alone.

Was this where he usually met with his mistress? she wondered, and felt her stomach turn over—felt the usual surge of bitter self-contempt begin to burn at how she let him get away with it.

Was it the mistress's turn to be unavailable?

The doors slid open on a private foyer. Sucking in a deep breath of air, she forced her unwilling limbs to start moving. Chin up as usual and her eyes revealing no hint of what was eating away at her insides, she stepped out of the lift and heard the doors hiss as they closed behind her.

But it was the man propping up a doorframe directly across from her who really held her attention. He was dressed casually in pale chinos and a white polo shirt that clung to the taut contours of his muscle-tight body. His big arms were folded across his wide chest, and one neat ankle crossed over the other. His lean, dark, frighteningly ruthless face was shuttered, his eyes hooded by long lush lashes as he looked her over.

'The hair,' he said.

That was all. Just 'the hair'. As she reached up in mute obedience to loosen the heavy flow of red-gold she saw the intensity with which he watched her fiery tresses tumble around her arms and shoulders.

It was a look she knew well and could feel it touch deep, deep in the very essence of her womanhood.

Desire, unhidden and unwanted.

It was time to begin again.

CHAPTER FIVE

IT SET the pattern for the next two months. When commuting to and from the island to Athens, Alex came to Mia's bed every night without fail except at weekends when, she presumed, he went to his mistress.

Mia told herself stubbornly that she didn't care, that the five days when he did come to her meant she deserved a brief respite on Saturday and Sunday from his insatiable demands on her.

Anyway, she always rang Suzanna on a Saturday morning and spent long, precious minutes reassuring the poor child that she had not been forgotten.

Those telephones calls hurt as much as they made each passing week bearable. The little girl was lonely. Mia knew what it felt like because she had been there herself during her own loveless childhood. She would usually spend the rest of the weekend sunk in the kind of heavy mood that made Alex's absence a relief.

During the day she had formed her own quiet routine where she swam twenty lengths of the pool before breakfast and the same again late in the afternoon. In between she read a lot, silently grateful that his home possessed such a comprehensive library.

Over the next three weeks Alex had her transported out to him on two occasions when he was away on business—once to Milan and another time to Paris. Each time she found herself being taken to the penthouse suite of one of his own hotels for a night of wild and wanton bedding.

She couldn't call it loving—*wouldn't* call it loving because what they shared was about as far away from that emotion as any two people could get.

At least during those brief trips away from the island they ate together—they talked to each other, even if it was a rather wary and constrained kind of talking. And the sex was different because he would not wait until she was safely lying in the darkness before coming to join her. He would undress her himself, and had her undress him. And sometimes—just sometimes—it would seem as if he almost cared for her a little, the way he would stand there in the middle of a bedroom and caress her with hands that almost seemed to revere the smooth, silken flesh they were touching.

And once during one of these much more intimate beddings that took place away from his private villa—times when he was warmer, kinder, much more attentive towards her, yet still managed to drive her into that mindless state of sensual fervour—he stopped when his body was lost deep inside her, pushed the wild strands of hair away from her face then lay there on top of her, his expression sombre.

'Why do you let me do this to you?' he asked.

Why? The answer almost escaped her kiss-warmed lips but she managed to bite it back. After all, how much mocking mileage would he make out of her admitting that she couldn't help herself?

'I don't know,' she replied honestly enough because she really did not know or understand why this man of all men should be able to move her so dramatically. 'What's your excuse?'

He sighed, something like that old self-contempt, which she had not seen in his face for a week now, clouding his lean, taut features. 'Like you, I don't know,' he answered heavily. For a moment, for a horrible gut-twisting moment, she thought he was going to withdraw from her and leave her in this high state of sexual need, the conscious acknowledgement of what they were doing here enough to cool his ardour.

But, far from withdrawing, what he actually did was bury

himself all the deeper inside her, his mouth trembling slightly as it came down to her own mouth. 'Whatever it is,' he muttered huskily, 'we may as well enjoy because once you are pregnant it will be over.'

It was a statement of intent. A *re-statement* of that intent issued to her, it seemed, so long ago now that she could barely recall the moment in her father's study when he had first made it.

It made their loving all the more urgent that night, made him come back to her time after time after time. The next morning, when she awoke to find him gone from her as usual, she was grateful for his absence, the pride-lowering fact that he never so much as acknowledged her during daylight hours for once a relief because she felt so utterly bereft, though she did not understand why that particular morning should be any different from all the others when she had woken alone like this.

Then the inevitable happened. Three and a half months into this marriage that wasn't really a marriage she missed her period.

Oddly, she said nothing. Oddly, she let him go on making love to her throughout the next four weeks until her second period failed to show itself. Oddly, she felt so terribly depressed by this second missed period that she was glad Alex was in the States again and therefore too far away to send for her for his habitual single night of passion to break up a business trip. Instead, she could use the time to come to terms with her own odd reaction to the one thing this had been all about.

A baby. They had managed to make a baby. A baby that was to make all her most secret dreams come true and would give Alex what he coveted most.

His island, his special piece of rock that lay out there somewhere among that cluster of tiny islands she could see from her bedroom window.

Will it all have been worth it? Mia wondered dully. All

this isolation she had endured, all the nights of loveless passion?

Oh, yes, she told herself flatly, it will have been worth it, and she grimly dismissed the way her heart coiled up tightly then throbbed as if it were hurting for something it had never been given the right to hurt for.

He arrived back at the villa late one afternoon while she was taking her usual exercise in the pool. She watched the helicopter fly over then disappear behind a bank of trees that acted as a wind-break to the pool area. As its rotor blades slowed in the warm still air she grimly returned to her exercise, pounding steadily up and down the pool with a stubborn resolve, refusing point blank to acknowledge any of the fluttering sinking sensations that were crawling around her insides.

She was just pulling herself out of the water when she glanced up to find him standing there.

It was a break from habit, and the irony of that break, coming now, did not escape her. He was still dressed for business in iron-grey trousers and a crisp white shirt, though his jacket was missing and his tie had been tugged loose. He looked tired, she saw. His eyes were hooded as usual as he ran them over her slender figure, encased in white clinging wet Lycra.

Already she was aware of the changes in her body, the extra heaviness in her breasts and their new excruciating sensitivity. She knew her waist was slightly thicker simply because her clothes felt tighter, and she was aware of a swelling around her abdomen that must show under the clinging swimwear.

It was therefore a purely defensive action that made her reach for a towel to cover herself, her eyes dropping away from his with guilt, embarrassment and a multitude of other things that didn't bear thinking about.

One of them was causing disturbance in the deepest parts of her body. It was desire, pure and simple. No matter who he was or what he was—or even why he was—she had grown to need him. She needed what he could do to her to make her lose her grip on the fierce self-control she had spent the best part of her life maintaining for one wretched reason or another.

Alexander Doumas, with his dynamic sensuality, had somehow managed to find a chink in her otherwise impenetrable armour, and in doing so had unwittingly made himself so indispensable to her new need to break free from her own constraints that she did not know how she was going to go on without him now it was, in effect, over.

And the worst thing of all, she acknowledged as she carefully wrapped the towel around her, was that knowing she felt like this about him had to be the most pride-lowering effect of the whole rotten bargain.

'I'm pregnant,' she announced, just like that without any preamble. It came blurting out because it had to be said before he had a chance to say the words she knew were about to come from him. She had seen the look in his eyes and had recognised it. He had been away for longer than a week, and if he had not been able to use the services of his mistress in that time then he had come to search her out like this because he needed her sexually.

If she'd hoped to jolt some kind of response from him by boldly announcing it like that, she failed miserably. Neither by stance nor expression did he hint at anything.

'Are you sure?' he asked quietly.

Her small chin lifted, her green eyes steady as they gazed into his. 'Yes.'

'How far?'

She gave a shrug of one sun-kissed, slender shoulder, and suddenly realised that she was going to have to admit that she'd let him go on taking her while she'd already suspected she could be pregnant. 'I missed my second period last week,' she told him with the usual defiant tilt to her chin. 'I w-wanted to be sure before I told you.'

It was a weak excuse but he made no comment. He just stood there and gazed at her in total silence, his eyes and his expression telling her absolutely nothing.

Yet she sensed in him something—something that kept her very still in the warm sunshine, held in breathless waiting suspense for...

For what? she asked herself confusedly.

Then she knew exactly what because when his answer came it struck so deep that it actually felt as if it might have made her bleed somewhere.

'That's it, then,' he said, and turned and walked away, leaving her standing there feeling cold, cast-down and rejected—feeling empty inside when, physically at least, she wasn't.

An hour later she was standing in her bedroom when she heard the helicopter take off again. With white face, clenched teeth, closed eyes and hands coiled into two tight fists at her sides, she stood there in the middle of the room and listened until the very last whirr of those rotor blades had fluttered into silence.

'That's it, then.' Those cruelly flat words had not stopped lacerating her since he had spoken them. There had been no enquiry as to her health—nothing but those three words that showed his contempt for both herself and their baby. Showed that the man had feelings cast in steel—he wanted the family island and did not care what he was forfeiting to get it.

She had expected nothing more from him but still the words had managed to cut her.

Then, quite without warning, the connecting door to his bedroom swung open. Mia started in surprise, whirling jerkily on her heel to find him standing where he should not have been.

The shock and confusion she experienced was so great that it sent her head spinning and the blood rushing from her brain to her tingling feet. Without really knowing why, since it had never happened to her in her life before, she quietly and silently sank into a faint.

'What the hell happened?' Alex's voice was curt, gruff, grating at her eardrums as she came round again to find herself lying on the bed with him standing over her, his dark face a fascinating mix of anger and concern.

'I thought you'd gone,' she whispered fraily. 'It w-was a shock when you walked in here.'

'You thought I'd gone?' He sounded so incredulous that she almost laughed. 'I've only just arrived. Why the hell should I want to leave again so quickly?'

'Why the hell should you want to walk into my bedroom during daylight hours?' Mia countered waspishly.

He shifted uncomfortably, his expression becoming closed as he dropped down to seat himself on the edge of her bed. 'I may be ruthless,' he muttered gruffly, 'but I'm not that bloody ruthless.'

It was such a small concession, such a very insignificant gesture on his part, that it really did not deserve the response it actually received yet...

Her arm came up, and of its own volition seemed to hook itself over his shoulder and around his neck as her eyes filled with weak, burning tears. She raised herself up and buried her face in the back of his shoulder—and wept.

Which of them was more shocked was difficult to determine. Mia was shocked at herself because, even in her darkest hours, she had never let herself do anything like this! She'd never cried in front of anyone—hardly ever let herself cry even in private—so she was shocked to find the flood-gates opening as abruptly as they did.

Alex was so shocked that he went rigid. She felt his shoulders grow tense, and his neck. She felt his heart thud against his ribcage as though the shock had jolted it out of its usual steady beat.

Then, with an odd, short, constrained sigh he was twisting around and putting his arms around her, holding her, saying nothing but allowing her to do what she seemed to need to do—to weep in his arms as though her heart were broken.

But, as with all impulsive gestures, this one had to come to an eventual end. When it did, when the sobs changed to snuffles and she became aware of just what she had done and with whom she had done it embarrassment washed over her in a wave. It coloured her damp cheeks and made her shudder in horror. She pulled away from him, scrambled off the bed and made her way to her bathroom, leaving him sitting there with his dark eyes following her.

She didn't look back, didn't want to know what was going on in those eyes. She wanted privacy while she came to terms with what had just taken place in that sunny bedroom.

For the first time in too many years to count Mia had reached out to another human being for comfort. She despised herself for her weakness. She hated him for making her this vulnerable to him. And she hated this whole horrible situation that should never have started, but which now had to continue on its set course.

It was a course which settled her into the next stage of limbo. Surprisingly, Alex did not walk away and forget all about her now his part in the deal they had struck was done. If he was in Athens he came home to the villa every evening. He even began to eat his meals with her, talking, spending the evenings with her. He took her out—picnics to quiet bays in the afternoons, or into Skiathos town during the evenings to enjoy a stroll along the busy L-shaped quayside, now bustling with golden-skinned tourists.

But, true to his word, he never came to her bed again. At night she would lie there, aware that he was lying in his own bed on the other side of that connecting door, and know that he would never cross that threshold again.

Another month drifted by and then another, and a doctor was transported from Athens on a regular basis to check her over. Her weight gain was swift, so much so that she was certain that if she did not keep up her exercise, by swimming twice daily in the pool, she would blow up like a giant balloon.

She didn't see the bloom on her face that seemed to glow with a secret kind of vitality or the way the rich redness of her hair had deepened, having a glossy sheen that shimmered like living fire in the sunlight.

She could not see how voluptuously alluring she looked, with her new maternal shape moulding the front of her body while the rest of her remained incredibly slender in every other way.

In fact, the one and only plus point she could find to all of this was that she loved her baby already. Although she might not like what he was doing to the shape of her body, she did not resent him doing it.

'You grow, my darling,' she whispered softly one morning, as she stood in front of the full-length mirror, ruefully viewing the physical changes while her fingers ran a gentle caress over her swollen abdomen. 'You take whatever you want from your mama to become the strong little man I want you to be.'

And he did take a lot, she had to admit. Took enough to see her safely tucked up in bed before ten each evening and resting several times throughout the day.

Then, on a Wednesday afternoon, two weeks into her fifth month of pregnancy, she was lying on her bed, resting, when she received a telephone call that put the energy back into her with a vengeance. Sofia had answered the call, then came running to get her.

'A Mrs Leyton?' She said the name with difficulty. 'She say it is urgent.'

Mrs Leyton—Cissy, her father's housekeeper—ringing here? Alarm shot through Mia, the kind of alarm that sent her legs to the floor and had her rushing down the stairs to the nearest telephone.

There were only two reasons why her father's house-keeper would be calling here—either something had happened to her father or something had happened to Suzanna.

Pray to God it isn't Suzanna, she begged as she lifted the receiver to her ear with a trembling hand.

It was Suzanna.

Ten minutes after that she was rushing around her bedroom, packing a small case, in a state of high turmoil.

'Listen, Elena,' she snapped at the hovering housekeeper for the very first time since she had arrived here. 'I have to go to England. I don't care how I get there, even if I have to swim! But I do have to go!'

'But the master says you are not to leave the island without him.'

'I don't damn well care what *the master* has said!' she bit back, lifting a flushed face and wild eyes from what she was doing. 'You must have some way you can contact him in case of an emergency! So contact him!' she commanded.

'Contact me for what?' a cool voice enquired from the open doorway to her bedroom.

Mia straightened from what she was doing and spun around to face him. 'Oh, Alex!' she sighed in relief. 'Thank goodness...'

'*Prosehe!*' she heard him shout as sudden dizziness overcame her.

She landed in an ungainly huddle on the bed beside her open suitcase, not unconscious but sickeningly close to it. Beyond the dizziness she could hear him still cursing, and was vaguely aware of him pushing the housekeeper out of the way in his urgency to reach her.

'You stupid, thoughtless female!' he growled at her angrily as he came to stand over her. 'When are you going to learn that you cannot exert yourself like this?'

'I'm all right now,' she whispered, through lips gone strangely numb.

'Oh, you look it,' he mocked grimly, watching the struggle it cost her to sit up again. 'Go any whiter and I won't be able to tell you from the sheet!'

'Just listen!' she cut across him, impatiently ignoring the lingering dizziness, the cloying sense of sickness disturbing her stomach. 'Suzanna, my s-sister, has been taken ill with acute appendicitis. I have to go to England,' she told him. 'She needs me.'

'She needs her father,' Alexander inserted coolly. 'You need to rest and take care of yourself.'

Was that a refusal? Mia glanced up at him and saw that his face was wearing that familiar closed expression. She felt her heart sink when she realised she had a battle on her hands. Elena, she noticed, had disappeared out of the firing line.

'She needs me,' Mia insisted.

Alex walked off towards the bathroom as if she hadn't spoken.

Mia got up, panic beginning to join all the other fears that were flurrying through her. 'Alex...' She met him at the bathroom door, her limbs still shaking and her head still whirling so dizzily that she had to clutch at the doorframe to steady herself. 'Please...' she pleaded with him. 'She's only seven years old! She's in pain and frightened! She needs me there to reassure her! I've always been there for her when she's needed someone!'

'Well, this time it will have to be someone else,' he declared, 'because you are not going. Here...' He offered her the glass of water he had gone into the bathroom to collect.

'I don't want that,' she snapped, and tried to spin away from him, but he stopped her, his free hand closing around her wrist.

'You are amazing, do you know that?' he bit out angrily. 'You walk around this place as if you live on a different planet to the rest of us! You rarely show emotion. You rarely raise your voice or make a move that has not been carefully thought out beforehand! You drift through each day as though you are not really living it. Then some stupid damned phone call comes, and you are suddenly so out of control that you are actually a danger to yourself!'

'What are you talking about?' She frowned at the anger blazing in his eyes.

'You—and the way you live here as if you do not really exist!' he barked. 'You...' his dark face came closer '...almost fainting because you are suddenly doing everything so thoughtlessly that it makes a damned mockery of all that self-control you usually exert over yourself! You!' he said forcefully. 'Almost making the same move just now that sent you toppling on the bed a mere moment ago! And all because of what?' he demanded. 'A sister who has a father to look to her comfort! A sister who can damn well comfort herself because you are not moving off this island!'

'But, you *know* my father!' she cried. 'Do you honestly think he would make time to bother visiting a child he barely remembers exists? She needs me, Alex! Me! And I have to go to her!'

'No.'

It was that blunt—so unequivocal that Mia let out a stunned gasp of appalled disbelief. He ignored it, as he ignored her pale, pained shattered face. He let go of her wrist to walk around her.

'In case you hadn't noticed,' he went on grimly, 'I am back here earlier than usual today because I thought you might enjoy a change of scenery.'

He was back early? Mia blinked at her watch and then blinked back at him, wondering confusedly what the hell that had to do with Suzanna.

'So I have arranged for us to eat a picnic out on a secluded bay I know on the other side of the island,' he continued off-handedly. 'Sofia is preparing the food for us as I speak.'

'I'm not going to sit quietly and eat some damned picnic while Suzanna needs me!' she gasped.

'You will, Mia.' It was so unusual for him to say her name that hearing it now made her blink again and stare at him—made her see exactly why he was using it. He was using it as a don't-push-me-or-I'll-get-nasty warning. 'You will do exactly what I say you can do. Your sister is not your concern.' he said. 'The child you now carry in your womb is your concern. Get your priorities right and forget you even received that phone call for, I promise you, it will be the last one you will receive from this moment on!'

'Oh, I see,' she said, her mouth turning down in a derisive sneer. 'The prisoner has now been placed in solitary confinement—is that it? I am not allowed off this stupid island in case someone guesses the shape of my body may have something to do with you! I am not allowed to speak to anyone outside these grounds in case I stupidly let them know my connection with you! Now I am not to receive phone calls from my own family in case they get the foolish impression that I still have a mind of my own to use now and then!'

'That's it...' he nodded '...in a nutshell. Now, do you want to swim while we are there? If so, pack some swimming gear.'

'I am not going with you!' she shouted at him.

His eyes narrowed, his dark head lifting as if she had just reached out and struck him. 'Don't speak to me like that,' he said, actually sounding shocked.

As an answer to that she walked over to her half-packed suitcase, closed it and hauled it off the bed.

She was a fool to try it, she knew that even as she attempted it. The suitcase was wrenched from her, the hand that came around her swollen body careful of the pressure it applied but demonstrating its intent none the less.

'Now, listen to me,' he said though gritted teeth from behind her. 'You signed a contract whereby I have more rights over you than you have over yourself. You are carrying my child!'

'Your passport to your most coveted dream, you mean,' she tossed at him. 'Other than that, I am nothing to you but the damned loss leader you had to accept if you had any chance of getting your hands on that stupid dream!'

'Loss leader?' he seemed rather stunned at her choice of phrase. 'You see yourself as a loss leader? What the hell do you think I am?'

'A cruel and heartless swine, if you keep me from going to a sick and frightened child who needs me!' she threw at him, and pushed his arm away from her, rather surprised when he let her do it. 'But, unlike you, I can't treat a child's pain and distress as nothing so I'm going—whether you like it or not!'

Reaching out, she snatched up her handbag and began to walk towards the bedroom door. Blow the case, she told herself grimly. She didn't need it. She had money of her own. She could buy fresh clothes when she needed them. She didn't need Alex. She could pay for her own passage off this damned island.

'I will not let you go, you know,' he informed her grimly.

'I am not aware of asking your permission,' she replied, as cold as ice and shaking so badly her legs could barely support her.

'My men will detain you the moment you approach the gates of the villa.'

She was at the top of the landing now, her hand clutching the banister, so she felt reasonably safe in spinning to face him without risking tumbling down those stairs in another silly faint.

He was standing several feet away, but was eyeing her calculatingly, as if he was wondering what she would do if he made another dive for her.

'Are you saying they will physically stop me?' she demanded.

'No,' he conceded, 'but I certainly will. Come away from

the edge of those stairs,' he commanded tersely. 'Your face tells me you are struggling to stay upright.'

'And your face tells me you have no idea whatsoever of what it is like to love someone more than you love your-self.'

'Are you talking about your sister?' he countered.

If anything, she went even paler. 'Yes,' she confirmed. 'Suzanna needs me. I am the only m-mother she has known all her life, and she has a right to expect me to come to her when she's hurting.'

'Go to her without my permission and you break your contract with me.'

Just like that. She stood there and stared at him.

Oh, so clever, she was thinking bitterly. He was calling her bluff. He was reminding her of the one tiny clause she had shown no interest in among all those other clauses he had thrust upon her in that contract—the clause that stated she not leave Greece without his permission while carrying his child or she forfeited custody of the child.

At the time of signing she had seen no reason why she should want to leave Greece until this ordeal was over.

Her heart gave a painful thump, her stomach muscles coiling in sickening understanding. It was time to choose—Suzanna or the baby growing inside her. A baby she loved already and would go on loving far more than this cruel man would ever love it.

Could she do that to her baby—forfeit all control over his little life to this man?

The rest didn't matter. The rest would happen, no matter what she did now. She was putting nothing else at risk but her baby's future.

My God, she thought bleakly, why does fate like to test me like this? Her eyes closed, her throat moving in a con-stricted swallow. As she hovered there, at the top of those polished stairs, she saw Suzanna's wan little face, looking up at her. Suzanna, with the same solemn green eyes as her own, with the same copper-red hair as her own and with the naturally vibrant personality that went with green eyes and red hair crushed out of her, just as it had been crushed out of Mia.

And, yes, she accepted, with an ache inside that almost sent her doubling up in agony, that she could forfeit this baby for Suzanna. She could do it simply because Suzanna had endured enough misery in her seven short years, whereas at least this baby would be allowed to be himself—that was one distinction she felt she could make between Alex and her father. Both might be despots, both might be ruthless and heartless, but Alex would not punish his son for the sins of the mother.

Mia's eyes fluttered open and looked into those darkly watchful ones. 'I h-have to go,' she whispered. 'I'm sorry.'

With that, she turned and walked down the stairs. Her heart was bleeding and her eyes were blurred by wretched tears because it was like history repeating itself and she didn't think she could bear it.

'Wait.'

She was at the bottom of the stairs before his command hit her eardrums. She stopped, shaking, frozen by the horrible fear that she was going to completely break down and give in to him if he put any more pressure on her.

His soft tread on the stairs as he came down towards her sounded like thunder inside her head. She didn't turn this time. She couldn't bring herself to face him because she knew her own face was showing such a conflagration of emotion that he would probably not understand it.

'Why?' he demanded roughly as he reached her. 'Give me one good reason why this so important to you, why you would throw away all rights to your own unborn child, and I will let you go to your damned sister!'

Her eyes fluttered shut, her heart squeezing in her breast on a pang of agony that only she would ever understand. Give him one good reason, he had demanded.

One good reason.

Well, she had one. 'Suzanna is not my sister,' she informed him unsteadily. 'She is my daughter...'

For the first time in seven years she had let herself say it, and it felt so strange that she shuddered.

'Is that a good enough reason for you?' she said into the bone-crunching silence that echoed around her.

CHAPTER SIX

NO ANSWER. Alex didn't say a single word and, after that, neither did she. Mia was trembling too badly to speak, anyway. She didn't know what kept Alex silent, and at that moment she didn't really care.

She was too shocked, dazed by her own admission and paralysed by the burning knowledge that, by saying what she had said, she had just lost Suzanna on a broken promise to another man.

Her father had warned her. It had been part of their bargain, written into that other contract they had signed between them. She was to tell no one of her true relationship to Suzanna before he had his precious grandson.

Now what had she got left? she asked herself starkly. She was standing here, ready to forfeit her claim over her unborn child, and had now, in effect, forfeited her claim over the one she had given birth to seven long years ago!

What did that make her? What kind of mother was she?

The hand was gentle on her wrist when it caught hold of her this time, but it was a mark of how badly she had shaken herself that she didn't even try to pull away from him.

'Come on,' he urged her huskily. 'It will take about an hour to get my plane to the airport here. Come and sit down while I make arrangements...'

He was treating her like someone would a highly volatile substance. She didn't really blame him. She felt very volatile, as though she might just explode with any more provocation.

It was a further mark of how weakened the ugly scene had left her that she allowed herself to lean against him a

103

little as he guided her across the hall and into the sunny sitting room. He saw her seated on one of the pale blue sofas then seemed to hover over her, as though he was preparing to say something.

Mia kept her eyes lowered and bit deep into her trembling bottom lip, waiting tensely for the questions to come.

Yet they didn't come. In the end Alex let out a small sigh and moved away—right out of the room, in fact—leaving her sitting there, still tense, still locked in the appalling fall-out of her own shocking confession.

Later—she wasn't sure how much later—Sofia arrived with a tray of tea-things, which she placed on a table in front of Mia, and then disappeared without a word.

More minutes ticked by. Alex came back and paused when he saw her sitting there just as he had left her. It was he who poured out a cup of tea for her and gently placed the cup and saucer in her hand.

'Drink,' he commanded.

She drank like an automaton. He stood over her, and once again she could sense the questions, rattling around his head. He wasn't a fool. He would already have worked out that if Suzanna was seven years old and Mia twenty-five then Mia had to have been very young when she'd fallen pregnant.

Seventeen years old, in fact. A small grimace touched her bloodless mouth as she lifted the cup to it. Seventeen, and her mother barely cold in her grave after killing herself in a car accident that was her own fault because she had been drinking. Her husband had driven her to look for escape from his mental cruelty in an alcoholic haze—which was still no excuse for leaving Mia alone with a father who hated her and a brother who couldn't care less about her.

So she'd rebelled.

And what a rebellion it had been, she mocked herself now and as bitterly as she had done ever since those wild six months after her seventeenth birthday.

She'd skipped boarding school. Run away. Had got in with a crowd of young groupies who'd followed the current rock group of the time around the country. It had taken the lead singer two months to notice her, a month to take her virginity and a another month to tire of her and throw her out of his life.

So there she had been—seventeen, homeless, penniless and pregnant. By the time Suzanna was born she had hit an all-time low, but it was still a very last resort that had sent her begging to her father.

'Drink some more.'

She glanced up to find that Alex was sitting on the sofa opposite. Her eyes quickly dropped away again, but not before they had taken in the fact that he had changed his clothes somewhere along the line. The business suit he had arrived home in had been replaced by something more casual in a pale linen fabric and a plain white T-shirt.

A sound outside brought her head up again. It was a car, drawing up at the front door. Alex stood up, came over to her and bent to remove her cup. 'Sofia has packed for us,' he murmured flatly. 'All we need to do is go now. OK?'

OK? Why was he asking her if it was OK to leave when he had never bothered to ask her opinion on anything before?

It didn't really matter now, she told herself hollowly as she nodded her head with its neatly styled hair, which should have drawn his anger but was a small detail that seemed to have passed by him unnoticed.

He went to help her rise to her feet again, but she withdrew abruptly from his touch. He was the enemy, she grimly reminded herself. You do not lean weakly on the enemy.

The journey to the airport was carried out in silence. The transfer to his private jet was achieved with the minimum of fuss, and it was only as she sat there, feeling the jet's

surge of power as it shot smoothly into the air, that it sank
in that Alex was actually sitting beside her.

'You didn't need to come with me.' She found her voice
at last, frail and constricted though it was. 'I will come back
just as soon as Suzanna is feeling better.'

He didn't answer. His lean, dark face was a closed book
as he sat there, gazing directly ahead. Not piloting the plane
himself this time, she noted. Not doing anything but sitting
here, lost deep within his own grim train of thought.

Tears filled her eyes. She didn't know why. They just
did. Then almost directly out of the rubble in which her
emotions lay, her chin rose in what had become a familiar
habit to those who had been around her during the last few
months. Her bloodless mouth straightened and her tear-
washed eyes cleared.

'I am not a whore.'

Why she said that was just as big a surprise to her as the
tears were that had preceded it.

'You announce yourself in those terms,' Alex quietly replied. 'I have never used the term to you.'

'You don't need to. I can hear it screaming at me every
time you look at me.'

From the corner of her eye she saw his grim mouth twist.
'You are your own salesman,' he said. 'Don't blame others
for believing what you place in front of them.'

Was that true? she wondered, then sighed because she
decided it was most probably very true and that she did
present herself as the kind of cool-headed mercenary who
would have sold her body for the proverbial pot of gold.

'Well, just in case you're worrying that I might have
passed on some dreadful social disease with my whoring
ways, I think I had better reassure you that there have only
been two men in my life who have used my body—Suzanna's father was one of them, and you the other.'

'If I had been worried about such a prospect I would
have insisted on the relevant test to reassure myself. As it

is...' his dark head turned to study her whitened profile
'...I already knew most of what you have just told me. I
had you thoroughly investigated, you see, before I agreed
to any of this. The nun's life you have been leading since
your wild rebellion eight years ago was easily discovered,
which made the way you responded to me all the more
intriguing...'

Her cheeks went red, and he lifted a finger to gently
stroke that heated skin. 'Only the fact that you have given
birth to a child escaped my investigators. Now that,' he
added softly, 'was a surprise.'

'And one you are now going to use against me, I suppose.'

'Will I need to?'

It was a challenge. Mia shivered delicately and shifted
her cheek so his finger had to drop away. 'I want my baby,'
she murmured huskily, 'but I will not keep him at
Suzanna's expense.'

'He doesn't warrant the same fierce feelings of love and
protection your daughter ignites in you?'

'Yes,' she admitted, one of her hands moving to rest on
that firm mound where her new baby lay. 'But Suzanna has
paid long enough for the misfortune of having me as her
mother. She deserves better and I am prepared to do anything to make sure I am in a position to give it to her.'

'Like sleeping with a man you hold in contempt?' he
suggested. 'Like taking any flak he might wish to throw at
you, without saying a thing in your own defence? Like
allowing yourself to be sent into isolation while he punishes
you for his own weaknesses?'

'So you acknowledge you have weaknesses?'

He smiled rather drily. 'I know myself quite well,' he
answered flatly. 'I know my weaknesses—and my
strengths. I am thirty-six years old, after all,' he added. 'If
I have not learned them by now then I truly am in danger

of becoming a man like your father. That is how you see me, is it not—as a man no better than your father?'

'You see a chunk of real estate as worth more than life itself so—yes,' she admitted. 'You are no better than him.'

'And you?' he challenged. 'What does that make you?'

Her green eyes flashed—the first sign of life they had shown since she'd walked away from him in that sunny bedroom back at the villa. 'I sold myself to you, not another's life.' She made the distinction. 'And you bought the use of me from my father, not from me. In return he gives you your precious island while he gets what he wants—a male heir to whom he can leave his filthy money. I get Suzanna and this child as payment. So the only thing I have sold to anyone is the use of my own body. You tell me what that makes me.' She threw the challenge right back at him.

His smile was cynical, to say the least. 'You seem to have conveniently forgotten the five million pounds your father is paying you on delivery of his male heir,' he drawled derisively.

Mia's heart-shaped upper lip clamped itself tightly to her much fuller bottom lip and she looked away from him out of the window at the clear blue stretch of sky through which they were flying.

The new silence pulled at the tiny muscles in her throat and around her heart, lining the wall of her tensely held ribcage.

'There is no money,' he bit out suddenly. 'You lied about the five million to throw me off the scent!'

'I have money of my own,' she countered defensively. 'I don't need money from my father.'

'Your mother's money.' He nodded, surprising her with just how deeply his investigators had dug into her life. 'She placed her money in a trust fund for you, which matured on your twenty-fifth birthday. A paltry two hundred thousand pounds,' he added with biting contempt.

Two hundred thousand was a small fortune to most people and more than Mia had ever had access to before. She could easily live off it with a bit of careful planning. She could bring her children up, know they would want for nothing materially.

'You know,' he muttered, 'you *are* a whore in a lot of ways.' With an angry movement he unfastened his seat belt and stood up. 'You sell yourself cheap and you see yourself as cheap!'

With that, he walked away, leaving her sitting there alone while she let the full thrust of his final angry words sink in.

It was getting quite late when they eventually landed, the August evening cool after the evenings Mia had grown used to back in Greece.

'Which hospital?' Alex asked her as they settled in the back of a chauffeur-driven Mercedes.

She told him, and he leaned forward to relay the information to their driver, who was separated from them by a tinted sheet of glass.

It was a small relief that he wasn't making a battle out of going directly to the hospital. She knew she was tired, and knew how that tiredness was showing on her pale, pinched face, along with the worry and strain she was experiencing for Suzanna's sake.

Suzanna. Her daughter. Her stomach flipped over, a frisson of anxiety shaking her system for that poor child she had never been able to claim as her own but who shared, none the less, the kind of bond with herself that really only a mother and child could share.

Mia might have been forced by circumstances to hand over her daughter to her father but he had never managed to break that bond, though he had tried—many times. 'She's my daughter now,' he had announced with grim satisfaction the day the adoption papers were signed. 'Ever be tempted to tell her who you really are and it will be the last time you will ever see her.'

Mia shivered as she sat there beside a silent Alex, remembering the choices she had been offered the day she went home to her father, frightened, desperate, destitute and carrying her new-born baby girl in her arms, to beg from the last man on earth she wanted to go crawling to.

'I won't have any gossip about my promiscuous daughter and her bastard child,' he'd warned her brutally. 'If you want my support, let me adopt her, though, God knows, I don't need another damned female hanging around me. You can be a sister to her,' he had decided, 'but as far as anyone is concerned she is my child, not yours, and don't you let yourself forget that.'

So she'd placed her own life on hold and had stayed living with her father so she could be close to her daughter. It was she who had brought Suzanna up since she was a baby, she who had seen to her needs throughout her young years, and she who had visited the child every weekend since her father had placed Suzanna in that dreadful boarding school. 'To toughen her up,' he'd announced heartlessly. 'The way you mollycoddle her, she will never learn to take care of herself if I don't split you up.'

But really he had sent Suzanna away to school because he knew how it would hurt the two of them to be separated like that. And because it placed Mia under yet more obligation to him. 'You can have her to yourself during the vacations,' he'd promised. 'So long as you remain living here with me, that is.'

Then Tony had been killed, and his whole attitude to both Mia and Suzanna had taken on a radical change. In Tony he had seen the continuance of himself. He hadn't needed to look any further for a male heir to his fortune. That was when Mia had become a tool for him to use for a different purpose—and Suzanna was the bait he had used to make Mia agree to everything he'd demanded.

'You get me a grandson and I'll let you have full custody of Suzanna. I'll choose the man. I'll discover the weak link that'll make him marry you. All you have to do is go to bed with him—not a problem for a whore like you.'

Not a problem. In the dimness of that luxury car she grimaced. Well, it hadn't been a problem in the end, had it? In fact, going to bed with Alex had turned out to be a pleasure! Which probably meant her father knew her better than she knew herself. Did he know she was already pregnant? Had Alex told him? She certainly hadn't. She'd had no contact whatsoever with her father since she'd got married. But Alex would have been eager to announce their success to Jack Frazier, she was sure.

In four more months or so her father would get the boy to whom he wanted to leave all his money, Alex would get his island and Mia would get custody of Suzanna.

All pacts with the devil, with this small baby growing inside her the unwitting champion for the three of them.

'Does she know you are her mother?'

The question made her jump, coming out of the blue as it did.

'No,' she replied. 'I am not allowed to tell her until this child is safely delivered.' Then her breasts heaved as she sucked in a tense breath of air and let it out again before she added huskily, 'I was not allowed to tell you either. If my father finds out that you know, he will say I have broken the contract I have with him and keep Suzanna, just for the hell of hurting me.'

The hospital came into view, its brightly lit windows announcing that time here had no real meaning. Work here went on twenty-fours a day.

Alex came with her, travelling through the corridors with a tight-lipped silence that kept his presence remote from Mia, who had become barely aware of him as her anxiety grew the closer they got to the ward to which they had been directed.

They came upon a nursing station first, with a pretty young nurse standing behind it who glanced up then smiled the warmest smile Mia had been offered in months. 'You must be Suzanna's sister,' she declared immediately. 'You look so much like her.'

'How is she?' Mia asked worriedly.

'Fine.' The nurse came around the station to touch her gently on the hand. 'The operation went off without a hitch. The appendix hadn't burst so she should have no complications. She's already out of Recovery and back on the ward here, though we do have her settled in a room off the main ward so we can keep a special eye on her.'

'Can I see her?' Mia's eyes were already darting off in the direction the nurse's hand had indicated.

'Of course. She's asleep,' the nurse warned as she moved off, with them following, 'but you can take a quick peek at her to reassure yourself. She has been asking for you constantly…'

The room was nothing more than a tiny annexe, with brightly painted pictures, done with childish hands, pinned all over the white-painted walls. But it was the little bed in the middle of the room that held Mia's attention. Her eyes darkened, her face losing what bit of colour it possessed as one trembling hand went up to cover the sudden quiver of her mouth while she stared at her daughter lying so pale and still.

Without taking her eyes off that sleeping face, Mia walked over to the bed, then gently stroked the child's pale cheek before she bent and replaced the hand with a kiss.

'She looks so vulnerable,' she whispered, worry-darkened eyes running over that little face with its shock of bright hair tied back to keep it tidy.

'She'll be sore for a few days,' the nurse said quietly, 'but she shouldn't feel too much discomfort. Her worst worry was that you wouldn't manage to come.'

Mia winced. Somewhere beyond the periphery of her own vision someone else winced also.

'Apparently, you were not in the country when she became ill.'

'I got here as soon as I could,' Mia said huskily. 'Has my father been in to see her?'

'No.' The nurse's tone cooled perceptibly. 'Only the lady who came in the ambulance with her. A Mrs Leyton—your father's housekeeper, I believe? She stayed until Suzanna was safely back up here again before she left.'

'Thank you,' Mia murmured. 'I'll sit here with her for a little while, if you don't mind.'

'Of course not,' the nurse said. 'There is a chair just behind you,' she added, and with a curious glance at the man who was standing in the far corner of the room, but who had contributed nothing to the conversation, she left them alone.

Mia didn't even notice. Her whole attention was fixed on Suzanna as one of her hands searched blindly behind her to find the chair so she could sit down on it.

Then she reached for and gently closed her fingers around Suzanna's small fingers, lifting them to her cheek and keeping them there. 'I'm here now, darling,' she murmured softly.

The child didn't move. She was still too heavily sedated to be aware of anything that was going on around her. But that didn't stop Mia talking gently to her, murmuring the kind of reassuring phrases a mother seemed to find instinctively.

Maybe the child did hear within the fluffy clouds of her own subconscious because something seemed to alter about her. Her slender limbs lost a tension that hadn't been apparent until it had eased away and her pale, rather thin face seemed to gain some colour.

As silently as he had observed everything, Alex observed the change in the child also, and just as silently he walked

out of the little room and left them to it, sensitive enough—
no matter how Mia believed the opposite about him—to
know he was intruding on something private.

He came back an hour later and, after pausing in the
doorway to frown at the look of exhaustion straining Mia's
features, he stepped forward and touched her shoulder. He
waited for and received the expected start that confirmed
to him that she had forgotten his presence.

'It's time to go,' he said quietly. 'We will return tomorrow, but you need to rest now if you don't want to end up
too tired to be of any use to her.'

A protest leapt to her lips—then hovered for a moment
before it was left unsaid. He was right, she conceded. She
was so utterly weary she could barely function. So, without
a word, she stood up, bent to the child's cheek then straightened, and without so much as a glance at him she turned
and walked out of the room.

As soon as she was settled in the car again her head went
back against the leather headrest and her tired eyes closed.

'You are very alike,' Alex remarked quietly. 'Does she
have your colour eyes, too?'

'Mmm.' Mia didn't want to talk—didn't even want to
think very much. Relief was, at this moment, playing the
biggest role in making her feel so exhausted. She had travelled from Greece to the hospital in a state of high nervous
tension, not knowing what she was going to find when she
got there. Now she had reassured herself that Suzanna was
going to be all right it seemed to make everything else
deflate inside her.

'Has no one ever made the natural connection between
the two of you?' Alex persisted. 'It seems impossible to
me not to consider a stronger bond than sisterhood when
the likeness is so strikingly obvious.'

'My brother had the same colouring,' she explained.
'People suspected Suzanna was my brother's child but not
mine because I was so young when I had her.'

'I thought you told me your father did not believe you were his daughter.' He frowned. 'But if you and your brother have the same colouring, surely he has to accept the blood connection somewhere?'

'We have the same mother,' she said. 'Exactly who it was that fathered us was a different thing entirely.'

'And a son was easier for your father to accept as his own than a mere daughter,' he concluded grimly, 'because it suited him to accept a son where, because of his bigotry, he didn't need to accept the daughter.'

'Now you're catching on,' Mia said very drily. 'If you want the full truth of it, I don't think my father is capable of fathering children,' she announced quite detachedly. 'More to the point, I think he knows it, which is why he set you and me up for this kind of deal when he could, at his age and with his money, have quite easily got himself another wife and produced a dozen more sons of his own. What's more,' she added, 'I think my mother was unfaithful to him from the day she married him.'

It was another confession that managed to shock her simply because she was actually telling it to Alex of all men.

'She came from a very socially acceptable family that had lost most of its money to inheritance tax. My father wanted to be accepted by that society so he bought himself into it, by marrying my mother. He wanted very socially acceptable sons to carry on his name for him, but when she didn't produce them he began to get nasty, calling her all those unpleasant names people can call women who don't have children easily. So she went out and got herself a lover. Conceived a child—though she was never absolutely sure whether either of her children belonged to her husband or her lover because she continued to sleep with both of them right up until the moment she managed to kill herself.'

'And the lover?'

'He died of cancer a couple of years ago,' Mia said, then

added reluctantly. 'He was Karl Dansing, the electronics magnate.'

There was a stifled gasp of shock from the man beside her. 'Are you trying to tell me,' he murmured gruffly, 'that you could be Karl Dansing's daughter?'

'Does that impress you?' Mia drawled. 'Well, don't go off the deep end about it,' she said mockingly before he could say anything further. 'As father figures go, neither impress me much. Karl Dansing must have known that Tony and I could have been his children but he never once owned up to it while he was alive, and didn't even give us a mention in his will.'

'But—.'

'Look—' She sighed wearily. 'Can we stop the inquisition, please? I'm too tired to deal with it and just too indifferent to want to talk about it! If you want to know anything else, put your investigators to work,' she suggested grimly. 'I'm sure they will come up with something juicy for you if you pay them well enough!'

With that, she closed her eyes firmly again, aware that she sounded embittered by her own sordid history. After all, who wanted to claim as parents the kind of people she had just described? She certainly didn't. Even spoiled, selfish, supremely avaricious Tony hadn't. 'I'll make do with what I've got,' he'd said to her once when Karl Dansing's name had come up. 'He may be worth a hell of a lot more than Jack but he has four other kids to share his money, whereas I'll be getting the whole lot from Jack one day.'

Only he hadn't got anything in the end, had he? Because Tony had died very much the same way their mother had died—in a car accident, while driving too fast with a skinful of booze and heaven alone knew what else.

She still missed him. Oddly and surprisingly, considering his selfish view of life. But they had shared a kind of affection for each other. And Tony had been good to Suzanna. In his own way she suspected he had even loved the child, which was enough for Mia to forgive him his other faults.

Suzanna...

Her mind drifted back to that poor, defenceless child she had left sleeping in her hospital bed. All at once depression swept over her. What was she going to do? she wondered fretfully. How was she going to bring herself to leave Suzanna again when Alex decided it was time to go back to Greece?

A more urgent question was how long he was going to let her stay here. A couple of days? A week? Maybe two, if she was lucky?

Whatever, it was not going to be long enough. Just seeing the little girl lying there had told Mia that Suzanna needed her to be closer to her!

It was the long vacation from school at the moment, which meant Suzanna would have to go back to her father's house when she was eventually discharged from hospital. The child couldn't cope with Jack Frazier on her own. She never had been able to. He only had to look at her to petrify her.

Cissy had told her during that hurried phone call today that her father had accused Suzanna of fabricating the pain in her side. He'd called it attention-seeking, and had told her that if she expected to get Mia back by playing on his sympathy then she was in for a disappointment because Mia was never coming back so she may as well get used to it.

Oh, God. How could one human being be so cruel to another? What had made Jack Frazier the cold hearted monster he was?

Her hand came up to rub at her eyes, where the ache behind them was beginning to drag at what was left of her severely depleted stamina.

Beside her, Alex moved. She went still, her nerve-ends beginning to sing beneath the surface of her skin because she had a horrible feeling he was going to reach out and touch her. If he did touch her, she was going to fall apart completely.

Then the car stopped and, bringing her hand away from her wary eyes, she found that his attention was fixed outside the car and not on her at all.

Which was a levelling experience, she discovered as she watched him open his door and climb out, impatiently waving the chauffeur away so he could come around the car and open Mia's door himself.

'You are almost dead on your feet,' he muttered, watching her sway slightly as she joined him on the pavement.

'I just need a good night's sleep,' she replied.

'What you need,' he grunted, as he helped her up the steps of a very exclusive white-painted town-house she presumed must be his home when he was in London, 'is to be yourself occasionally, and not all these other personalities you conjure up, depending on who it is you are having to deal with!'

'Oh, very cryptic,' she mocked.

'Not cryptic—tragic,' he corrected grimly. 'A good psychoanalyst could make a life study out of you,' he muttered, stabbing an angry finger at the front doorbell. 'Today alone I have met the vixen, the ruthless negotiator, the loving mother and the cynic,' he said, with tight-lipped sarcasm. 'As the old saying goes, would the real woman please stand and reveal herself?'

'Not for you she won't,' she tossed back frostily.

'Oh, I've already met her,' he insisted tightly. 'In her bed, in the darkness. And she is quite the most fascinating one of all, I assure you.'

'You're mistaken,' Mia replied. 'That was the whore you met there— Why are you ringing this bell, instead of using a key to get in the house?' she asked frowningly.

'Because—obviously—the house does not belong to me,' he replied sardonically.

The front door swung open, and she was suddenly faced with exactly whose house this was.

Oh, hell! she thought wearily. What now? Why this? What was it supposed to mean?

It was Alex's younger brother, Leon.

The front door swung open, and she saw suddenly faced
with empty, silent house that was
Oh, hell, she thought wearily. What now? Why then?
What was it supposed to mean?
It was Alex's v

CHAPTER SEVEN

'AH,' LEON smiled politely enough. 'So you are here at
last. We were beginning to give up on you.'

But Mia could see by the way his eyes barely touched
her that he was no happier to see her standing on his door-
step than she was to be here. He obviously still resented
her intrusion into Alex's life, and was not going to bother
to hide it.

'Come on in,' he said.

Her shoulders drooped wearily, the long, long day spent
enduring all the other stresses leaving her with nothing with
which to fight this next ordeal.

An arm came warmly about her shoulders, and for once
she huddled gratefully into it, going into retreat because it
was the only thing she could do as Alex propelled her into
a warmly lit hallway then paused to murmur something to
his brother in his own language.

She didn't know what he'd said—didn't want to know—
but she sensed the hint of a warning beneath the casual
tone and the arm around her shoulders tightened briefly, as
if to offer support.

With what she suspected was a forced lightness, Alex
enquired rather drily, 'Where's the wicked witch?'

'I heard that,' a sharp female voice responded.

What now? Mia wondered, raising very wary eyes to see
the most exquisite vision of blonde loveliness, dressed in
tight faded jeans and a skinny white top, appear at the top
of the stairway in front of her.

Very tall and incredibly slender, she had the bluest pair
of eyes Mia had ever encountered but what was most dis-

concerting was that those eyes were smiling at her warmly—genuinely warmly.

'Hi,' she said pleasantly. Then, before Mia could answer, she went on, 'Oh, good grief, but you look dreadful! What's the matter with you, Alex?' She frowned at him. 'Trailing a pregnant woman all over the world, as if she's some piece of baggage! How is your sister?' she asked Mia, without waiting for Alex to answer either. 'Is she very poorly? Mia, isn't it?' She smiled that warm smile again. 'I'm Carol,' she announced. 'The lucky one because I got the nicer brother. You drew the short straw, I'm afraid, when you got Alex.'

'Mia is exhausted,' Alex interrupted rather irritably. 'She doesn't need all your crazy chatter right now. She needs her bed.'

'Oh, sorry,' Carol said, sounding rather disconcerted by his curt tone. 'This way, Mia. Gosh, you look done in. Will you let me help you? You can lean on me, if you want to. I don't mind.'

'I can manage, thank you,' Mia answered quietly.

'Yes. Right.' Carol nodded, and after a short pause, when she glanced from one brother to the other, she turned and began to lead the way up the stairs while Mia followed, having to draw on the very last dregs of her stamina.

She was shown into a prettily decorated bedroom, with blue walls and apricot furnishings. There was a connecting bathroom, where Carol took it upon herself to run Mia a bath while all Mia could do was lower herself onto the side of the bed and wilt.

By the time Carol came back into the bedroom Mia knew all about Leon, the great love of Carol's life. How they met, where they met and where he had proposed to her. She now knew that they had been married for two years but were not going to start a family yet because Leon had insisted that his children were born in Greece and they couldn't go and live in Greece until the new hotel they had just bought and were refurbishing here in London was finished up and running.

'The bath's ready,' Carol announced. 'All you have to do is get undressed and sink into it. I'll be back in half an hour to make sure you're all right...'

Silence. At last a blessed, beautiful silence fell upon the room at her exit. Mia remained where she was for a few precious minutes and simply let that silence flow all around her, then made herself get up and trail her weary body into the bathroom.

By the time she had hauled herself in and out of the bath again she was so utterly worn out that she had to sit down on the bathroom stool to recover. Hell, she thought as her head began to swim, a quick shower would have been more sensible in your condition. You really should have known that!

'How are you doing in there?'

Carol was back already, Mia noted wryly.

'One moment,' she called back, hurriedly donning the short white silk slip-style nightdress Carol had thoughtfully hung behind the bathroom door for her. She ran a quick brush through her hair and, on a deep fortifying breath, let herself out of the bathroom.

'Wow!' the other woman gasped. 'Look at all that hair! You're gorgeous, aren't you? No wonder Alex has been walking around looking as though he doesn't know what's hit him! I hope my figure looks as good as yours does with a bump stuck on the front of it. Here, get into bed. You'll be more comfortable there...'

Without a word, Mia did as she was told. A tray landed across her lap. Her pillows were fluffed up.

'Now...' Standing back to view her ministrations, Carol frowned and then smiled when she realised she was frowning, as though she was trying very hard to make Mia feel wanted. 'I'm going to leave you—Alex's orders.' She grimaced. 'He's frightened I'll say something I shouldn't—

like I think its disgraceful the way he's been treating you, no matter what the circumstances. See?' She grinned. 'I've said it anyway!'

Not that she seemed to care!

At last she disappeared. Mia wilted again, and in the next second her mind switched off. As if it had taken more than enough for one day and was refusing to accept any more, it dropped her into a slumber from which she didn't even stir when the bedroom door opened again an hour later.

Alex stood on the threshold, staring at the way she had fallen asleep, half sitting up and with the untouched tray still lying across her lap.

With stealth he closed the door, then moved across the carpet to stand over her. She looked exhausted, even in sleep, the signs of stress evident in her washed-out face. Without disturbing her, he removed the tray and set it aside. Then, after another brief grim study of her, he turned and walked into the bathroom.

Ten minutes later he was back, showered, shaved and wrapped in a thin black cotton bathrobe. Silently he moved around the room, switching off several lamps Carol had left burning. Then, with the darkness enfolding him, he came back to the bed, removed the bathrobe and slid his unashamedly naked body into the bed beside her.

Still she did not so much as move a muscle. He lay there on his side and watched her for ages before—on a grimace that said he didn't much fancy what he was about to do next—he leaned over her so he could slide an arm beneath her shoulders and lift her just enough to remove one of the pillows from behind her.

As he settled her back again in what he hoped was a more comfortable position her eyes flickered open, green homing directly onto guarded brown.

Mia blinked slowly, her sleep-sluggish mind taking its time to remember that it had been long months since she had woken to find him leaning over her in the darkness like this.

As she did remember, her eyes widened warily.

'It's OK,' Alex said softly. 'I was not about to seduce you while you were sleeping. I was simply trying to make you more comfortable.'

'What are you doing here?' she whispered, still staring owlishly into those rich, dark, slightly rueful eyes of his.

'Carol's idea,' he said. 'She naturally assumes we share a bed, and I was not up to one of her question-and-answer sessions, by informing her that we did not.'

Grimacing, he moved away from her, going to lie on his back and stare at the ceiling while Mia took a few moments to take in this totally unexpected new situation.

He intended to share her bed, she seemed to find it necessary to tell herself. They had been married for almost seven long months, and *never* shared the same bed as a married couple normally did.

Now this. It felt weird, like lying next to a stranger.

'Do you mind?' he asked quietly.

'Its a big enough bed.' She shrugged. 'I suppose we will manage.'

Silence fell, the kind of tight, stinging, uncomfortable silence that caught at the breath and increased the tension in the darkness of the room.

'Why did you bring me here to your brother's house?' Mia asked when she could stand it no longer.

'It is the *family* house,' he said. 'Leon and Carol are in residence right now because Leon is based here at the moment. They expect me to stay with them when I am in London. It would have been...awkward if I had taken you to a hotel.'

'I won't do or say anything that could embarrass you,' she assured him huskily.

His dark head turned. Mia felt his eyes on her. 'You have a very low opinion of me, don't you?' he said.

Mia's head turned so that their eyes clashed again. 'It's mutual,' she countered.

He didn't answer, those lush, long, coal-black lashes flickering slightly as he continued to lie there studying her in the darkness—a darkness they had always been more comfortable in. A darkness where most of their most intimate moments had taken place—their mutual passion, their ability to drown in each other.

Drown, as Mia could feel herself beginning to drown right now—drown in those deep, dark, sensually knowing eyes that could probe right inside her and touch places only this man had touched, ignite senses only this man could ignite.

'Go to sleep,' he ordered softly.

Sleep. Yes, she agreed, dragging her eyes away from his. Don't look at him, she told herself sternly as she turned her head on the pillow. Don't even think about him, lying here next to you.

And don't, for goodness' sake, remember what it feels like to have him make love to you!

The stern lecture made no difference because she did imagine him making love to her. She could feel his hands caress her body, feel his mouth move sensually on hers, could feel her breathing growing shallow as her heart picked up pace and that place between her thighs begin to pulse with a message so erotic that she had to lie very still with her muscles tightly clenched in an effort to subdue the feeling.

What made it all worse was that it was all happening under his steady gaze. She could sense him watching her, knew he was witnessing the increase in her breathing and the way her eyes couldn't close because she was holding herself so tense beside him. A tension that was fizzing in the air around them. Sexual tension.

'Go to sleep,' he repeated in a soft, silken voice that

utterly rejected every message her stupid body was sending him.

Dismayed, she threw herself onto her side and away from him, so agonised by her own weaknesses that it actually hurt like a physical pain.

It took her ages to relax and ages to drift back into a restless slumber—only to come blisteringly awake again the moment she felt him move beside her.

With her heart beginning to pound in her aching chest, she listened to him release a heavy sigh then carefully slide out of the bed. There was a rustling sound as he pulled a robe over his body. Even in the darkness, with her back towards him, she could feel his grimness and knew—just knew—that the grimness was there because he hated this situation so much.

Hated having to lie here beside her in this bed when he was probably wishing himself a million miles away.

With his mistress, most probably.

He threw himself down in one of the easy chairs by the curtained window. She heard him sigh again, then—nothing. Nothing for long minutes while she held herself still, listening until she could stand to listen no longer and turned over in the bed to gaze at the dark bulk by the window.

He was asleep, stretched out in the chair with his dark head thrown back and his face a mask of grim perseverance.

Tears began to burn at the back of her eyes. Weak tears. Wretched tears. Foolishly hurt tears! She fell asleep like that, with the tears still clinging to her lashes.

When she awoke next morning she was alone as usual. The knowledge that Alex had found it impossible to spend a whole night in the same bed with her lay like a lead weight across her chest.

Then she remembered Suzanna and got up, showered quickly and dressed herself in a pair of comfortable stretch white leggings and a pale blue overshirt, before taking a deep breath and letting herself out of that bedroom to go in search of the others.

She was just coming down the stairs when Alex walked out of one of the rooms off the hallway. He saw her and paused to watch her descent through those impenetrable brown eyes of his.

'You still look tired,' he observed huskily.

Still stinging from last night's humiliating rejection, she dropped her eyes from his and concentrated fiercely on the stairs in front of her. 'It's worry, not tiredness,' she contended. 'I would like to ring the hospital,' she went on coolly. 'Is there a telephone I could use?'

'Of course.'

Stepping back to the room he had just walked out of, he opened the door and gestured her through it. She found herself standing in a study that was very male in style—a lot of polished wood, walls lined with books and the more modern state-of-the-art communications hardware.

There was a desk by the window, with a telephone sitting on it. Mia thanked him quietly and walked over to pick up the receiver.

Her thanks had been a polite way of dismissing him but, to her annoyance, he didn't leave her to her privacy but came to lean on the desk beside her so he could watch her face while she spoke to the hospital.

Suzanna had spent a comfortable night, she was assured. She also knew that Mia had been in to see her late last night, and the fact that she was actually here in London had cheered the child up remarkably. 'She keeps on asking when you are coming in again,' the nurse told her.

'Later this morning,' Mia replied. 'Tell her I will be with her just as soon as I can be.'

'OK?' Alex asked quietly as she lowered the receiver.

Mia nodded, her lips pressed together to stop them from trembling, but it still hurt to think of that little girl spending the whole of yesterday sick and in pain and probably very frightened of what was happening to her.

'Then what is the matter?' he asked. 'You look almost— hunted.'

'I'm fine,' she lied. 'I n-need to ring my father next, that's all.'

'Ah,' he said, as if that explained everything. 'Would you prefer me to make that particular call for you?' he offered.

Instantly her chin lifted and her eyes met his with their usual defiance to give him his answer. He smiled wryly. 'You trust me about as much as you trust him, don't you?'

Mia didn't answer—didn't need to. He knew exactly how little she trusted him.

The housekeeper answered her call. The moment she heard Mia's voice she went off on a harried burst of speech that showed just how anxious she had been about Suzanna.

Mia listened with her eyes lowered and her fingers clenched. Her knuckles were white around the receiver as she strove to contain the black anger that was building inside her.

For three days Suzanna had been complaining of pain— and for three long, wretched days her father had cruelly dismissed the child's distress as a ploy to bring her precious Mia back.

Her eyes began to flash and her heart to pump on an adrenaline rush. Beside her, Alex shifted his position a little, catching her attention and bringing those green eyes flashing upwards to pierce him with enough burning venom to make his own blink.

'No—no, Cissy,' she murmured smoothly, in reply to whatever the housekeeper had said to her. 'I'm right here in London. I visited Suzanna last night, and I'm going back to the hospital this morning so you don't have to worry about her now.'

Another volley of words hit her burning eardrums and

Mia had difficulty containing what was screaming to be released inside her.

Alex brought a hand up to grab her chin, then tugged it around in his direction. His eyes were black, boring into hers with stunned fascination. 'My God,' he breathed. 'You're cracking up! The ice is beginning to melt at last!'

'Is my father there?' she asked the housekeeper in a voice as cool and calm as a mill pond on a winter's day, while her eyes spat murder into those probing black ones. 'Can I speak to him, please?'

Cissy told her that her father had meetings all day and that he had left the house very early, without even bothering to ask after Suzanna. Why? Because the child held no great importance in the real plan of things! She was simply a very small pawn he used to make Mia jump to his bidding.

Another loss leader.

It was cruel, it was sick and it was downright criminal. By the time Mia replaced the telephone she was shaking like a leaf and ready to hit out at the nearest person.

Alex.

Angrily she turned away from him, her slender arms wrapping around her own body in an effort to contain what was desperately clamouring to burst free.

'Mia—'

'Say one more word,' she bit out, 'and I am likely to spoil your handsome features!'

There was a choked gasp from behind her. 'What did she say to you?' he demanded roughly.

'Nothing you would find unacceptable,' she retorted. Then, because she knew she needed to calm down because she could feel the usual dizziness surging up to pay her back for allowing herself to get this agitated, she took a jerky step towards the door. 'I need to—'

'No!' The hand that closed around her wrist stopped her from going anywhere. 'I want to know what she said to make you so angry,' Alex insisted grimly.

Mia rounded on him like a virago. Her teeth bared and her eyes spitting green fire, she hit out at him with her free fist. It missed its target because he ducked out of its way—which in turn sent her off balance so she stumbled and would have fallen if he hadn't caught her to him.

'What the hell was that for?'

'Three days!' she choked out. 'She was ill for three whole days before my father condescended to let Cissy bring in a doctor!'

'And you think I could be that callous?' He looked white suddenly—white with anger. 'I am *not* your damned father!' he railed at her furiously.

No, she thought, you are just the man who is breaking my heart in two! 'Oh, God,' she said brokenly when she realised just what she was telling herself. 'Let go of me,' she whispered, feeling the all too ready tears beginning to build inside.

Maybe he sensed them threatening—certainly he could feel the way her body was trembling as he was holding her so close—because, on a driven sigh, he let go of her. 'You should not let yourself get upset like this,' he muttered. 'In your present condition it cannot be good for you.'

Ah, her present condition. Mia allowed herself a tight smile. 'I'm fine,' she said grimly, pulling herself together. 'It's my sister's health that worries me, not my own.'

'Your *daughter*,' he corrected.

'Sister,' she repeated. 'She will not be my daughter again until I have safely delivered this child I am carrying now.'

Alex came with her to the hospital that morning, though Mia wished he could have shown a bit of sensitivity and let her have this first very painful meeting with Suzanna alone.

As it was, the child took one look at her as she walked in the room and dissolved into a flood of tears. Mia just gathered her gently into her arms and held her there, struggling hard not to weep herself.

'Daddy said you wouldn't come,' the child sobbed as she clung to her. 'He said you didn't want me any more because I'm a nuisance.'

'That's not true, darling,' Mia murmured reassuringly. 'You will never be a nuisance to me and I will always come if you need me. Always. Didn't I promise you that the last time I saw you?'

'But he said you'd gone away to start your own family!' the child sobbed out accusingly. 'S-so I'd better get used to you not being around! But I missed you, Mia!'

It was a cry from the heart that cut so deep even Alex, a silent witness to this tragic overload of emotion, could not stay silent any longer.

'Hello,' he said, stopping Suzanna's tears as if he'd thrown a switch.

Her face came out of Mia's shoulder so she could look towards that deep, smooth, very male voice, first in surprise because she hadn't noticed him come in with her precious Mia and then with all the natural wariness of a child towards any total stranger.

A very tall, very dark, very handsome stranger, who was smiling the kind of smile that made Mia's heart flip because she recognised it as the same smile he had once used on her—before her father's bargain had effectively killed it.

'My name is Alex,' he introduced himself. 'Mia is my wife.'

Wife. Her heart flipped a second time. He had formally acknowledged her as his wife for the first time ever, and the word seemed to echo strangely inside her head.

Like a lie that wasn't quite a lie but still sounded like one nonetheless.

'And you are Suzanna…' With each gently spoken word he came closer, holding Suzanna's attention like a hovering hawk mesmerising a wary rabbit. He came down on his haunches beside the bed where Mia was holding the child against her. 'I am very pleased to meet you.'

He offered Suzanna his hand in greeting. Her tear-spiked lashes flickered to the hand, then uncertainly back to his face again—before finally looking to Mia in search of some hint as to how she should respond.

Don't ask me, Mia thought drily. I still haven't worked that one out and I've been living with him for months. She smiled reassuringly. 'It's OK. You can like him. He's nice.'

'Thank you,' Alex murmured in a dry undertone that said he'd caught the mocking intonation behind the remark.

By then Suzanna was cautiously placing her little hand in his, and Alex's full attention was back on the child.

It was a revelation, simply because Mia had never known he had it in him, but within minutes Suzanna had forgotten her tears, forgotten her woes. In fact, she seemed to have forgotten everything as, with amazing intuition, Alex breached the little girl's natural shyness with men in general by encouraging her to describe—in lurid detail—every stage of her emergency dash to the hospital in an ambulance and the ensuing course of events that had led to her waking up here in this bed with stitches in her tummy.

'They're horrid,' she confided. 'They hurt when I move.'

'Then try not to move too much,' advised the man, whose simple logic seemed to appeal to the child.

'Thank you,' Mia murmured gratefully an hour or so later, when Suzanna had drifted into a contented sleep.

'For diverting her mind from the horrors your father has fed into her?' He got up from the bed where somehow he had managed to swap places with Mia so she had ended up seated more comfortably on the bedside chair. 'That does not require thanks,' he stated grimly. 'It requires defending.'

He was right. It did. Mia didn't even take offence at the comment. 'He is not a nice man.' She sighed. 'He likes to control people. You, me, Suzanna—anyone he can gain power over.'

'Which does not justify her being treated to that kind of mental torture,' Alex countered harshly.

Mia went pale, but she nodded in agreement. 'Maybe now you can understand why I had to marry you. I had to do what was necessary so I can remove her from his influence.'

'An influence she should never have been exposed to in the first place!'

They had been talking in low voices by necessity in such close proximity to the sleeping Suzanna, but those words cut so deep into Mia's bones that she could not sit still and take them on the chin as she really knew she should do.

She got to her feet and walked right out of the room on legs that were shaking so badly they could barely support her.

When Alex eventually came looking for her he found her standing in the corridor, staring out of one of the windows that overlooked the hospital car park.

'I'm sorry,' he said heavily as he came up behind her. 'I did not mean to sound so critical of you. It was your father I was condemning.'

She didn't believe him. 'You think I am the lowest of the low for handing my child over to him,' she murmured unsteadily. 'And don't think that I don't know it!'

'That is your own guilty conscience talking,' he said with a sigh. 'I only wish you could have told me from the beginning why you had been forced to agree to this marriage!'

'What was I supposed to say?' she said cynically. 'Oh, by the way, I'm doing this because I had another child but I gave her away and this is the only way I can get her back again?' Her eyes flashed, her cheeks blooming with anger. 'That would really have made you respect me, wouldn't it?'

'And you want my respect?' he asked huskily.

Her heart hurt with the truthful answer to that question. 'I just want to get through these next few months without falling apart,' she answered shakily.

Silence greeted that, a grim kind of silence that held them both very still in that hospital corridor. Alex stood behind her, a dominating force as he stared over her shoulder at the car park beyond.

Mia felt like crying. Why, she didn't know—except maybe it had something to do with the need pounding away inside her breast that wanted her just to turn around and throw herself against the big, hard chest behind her.

'Do you have copies of the adoption documents?' Alex asked suddenly.

She steadied her lips and nodded. 'Yes,' she whispered.

'Where are they?'

Mia frowned at the question and turned to face him. 'I keep them with my other papers in my vanity case back at the villa in Skiathos,' she told him. 'Why?'

'Because I would like to see them, if you have no objection.'

No objection? Of course she had objections as a sudden fear drained her face of its colour. 'You want to use them against me, don't you?' she accused him shakily. 'You think that if I gave my child away once then a court of law would not give me custody of a second child! You—'

'You,' he cut in angrily, 'have a nasty, suspicious, insulting mind!' He was so very right!

'And that makes you feel very superior to me, doesn't it?' she flashed back hotly. 'Well, let me tell you something, Alex. I won't ever think you superior to me while you go on believing that a lump of rock somewhere in the Aegean is more important to you than your own DNA!'

CHAPTER EIGHT

ALEX rocked back on his heels as if Mia had struck him. He looked frighteningly angry and Mia couldn't breathe— she didn't dare to in case she released whatever it was she could see threatening to explode inside him. Her heart began to hammer, the world beyond his stone-like stance blurring at the edges. Then he moved, and so did she, sucking air into her starved lungs on a tension-packed gasp.

What she'd thought he'd been about to do to her she had no idea, but when he turned on his heel and strode away she stared after him with horror that verged on remorse.

Because it hit her—really hit her as she watched him go—that she had just inadvertently struck at the very heart of him, though she did not know how or with what!

When she was ready to leave Suzanna, after eating her tea with the little girl, it was Carol who appeared in the doorway to the little room.

'Oh, you have to be Mia's sister because you are like two peas from the same pod!' she declared, making Mia jump nervously and scan the empty space around Carol in the flesh-tingling fear that Alex would be there.

He wasn't. For the next ten minutes Carol talked Suzanna into a blank daze as she produced, during her mindless chatter, little presents from the capacious black canvas bag she'd had slung over her shoulder when she arrived.

A pocket computer game. 'From Alex,' she explained to Suzanna. 'He thought it may help to fill the time in when Mia has to rest. She's making a baby—did you know she's making a baby?'

Suzanna gave a nod about the baby, whispered a thank-you for the computer game and stared at the beautiful Carol with something close to star-struck idolisation as the other woman chatted on as if they'd known each other all their lives.

'Now, I've been ordered by Uncle Alex to take Mia home and make her rest,' Carol informed her latest conquest, 'so she can be fresh as a daisy when she comes back here tomorrow.'

'Will you come, too?'

Mia felt the wall around her heart crack, oozing a warm, sticky liquid called heartache for this child of hers who was so hungry for this kind of warm affection.

'I'll be coming to collect Mia after I've finished work.' Carol nodded.

When Mia bent down to receive her goodnight kiss the little girl clung to her neck. 'You will come back again, won't you?' she whispered anxiously.

'Tomorrow morning,' Mia promised.

'What did you say to put Alex in such a bad mood?' Carol asked the moment they were inside her car. 'He's been stomping around the hotel like a demolition man all afternoon.'

'You work there, too?' Mia asked in surprise.

'You think I'm a real blonde bimbo, don't you?' She grinned. 'I'm not, you know. I am an interior designer. I work on all the Doumas projects.'

She changed gear with a flourish and changed lanes with the deftness of someone who was used to taking on London rush-hour traffic.

'It's called keeping it in the family,' she explained. 'Leon is the construction expert, Alex the one who makes every new project pay. We are in a rush to get this one in London completed so we can start on the island project once you've had this baby. Only the island will be a private renovation,' she explained, oblivious or just completely indifferent to the way Mia had stiffened up at the fact Carol knew exactly why Alex had married her.

'The house has been left to decay while your father has been in possession. The land around it has turned back to scrubland that only goats find idyllic. Once it was a beautiful place...' she sighed wistfully '...and we intend to return it to its former glory. Now you know that I know exactly what goes on between you and Alex, will you tell me what you said to upset him?'

'None of your damned business,' Mia said abruptly, feeling angry, bitter and utterly, cruelly betrayed. And, worse than all that, feeling as if every rotten word she had thrown at Alex earlier had just been well and truly justified!

'Since you seem to know *all* my business,' she added angrily, 'do you think I could have a bedroom of my own, please? Knowing it all must surely mean that you also know that Alex never sleeps in my bed! So let's make life easier for him and give him his very own bed in his very own room so he doesn't have to spend the night stretched out in the chair in my room!'

'Oh my...' Carol drawled after a long taut silence. 'I think I've put my big mouth in it again! Did he really sleep in the chair?' She had the cheek to giggle. 'That'll teach him not to play mind games with his next of kin!'

'I don't know what you're talking about,' Mia said crossly.

'I know,' Carol laughed. 'That's what makes it all so amusing!' The car pulled to a stop outside the white townhouse. 'Are you sure you want a separate bedroom?' she goaded teasingly. 'He's supposed to be a dynamic lover—so rumour has it. Won't you miss him slipping between your sheets to have his evil way with you?'

Too angry to care any more, Mia retaliated spontaneously. 'You have it all wrong,' she snapped, grappling for the car door lock. 'He will still slip between my sheets when the mood takes him. He just does not approve of spending the whole damned night with a whore, that's all!'

As an exit line it was perfect, except she had nowhere to exit to. She hurled herself out of the car, certainly, but she had to stand by the closed front door and wait until Carol opened it with her key before she could make her real exit.

'I'm sorry,' Carol murmured as she stepped up beside her, and for once the other girl sound genuinely subdued. 'Believe it or not, I wasn't trying to offend you,'

No? Mia thought. Well, you could have fooled me!

'I was, in actual fact, teasing you at Alex's expense,' she admitted ruefully. 'He was the one who insisted that you share a bedroom, you see...'

Which meant—what? Mia wondered. That he was attempting to save face in front of his family? Well, if that was the case, he should have kept his mouth shut about the rest of their arrangements, shouldn't he?

'Do you have a key for this door or do we stand here until someone arrives who does?'

'I have a key.' Carol sighed, and fitted it into the lock, then pushed open the door. 'Mia—'

But Mia was already stalking towards the stairs and so furious she was barely managing to contain it.

'He's going to kill me if I have to confess what I've said to you!' Carol cried pleadingly after her.

'Good,' Mia said between gritted teeth. 'Do me a favour and kill each other—it will solve all my problems for me if you do!'

'This isn't a joke!' the other girl shouted.

Then Mia did explode, turning round at the base of the stairs to glare back down the hallway. 'You're right it's no joke!' she cried. 'I am seriously having his baby! And he seriously impregnated me to get it! So don't you dare make a mockery out of— Oh,' she groaned as the hall began to swim around dizzily.

The next thing she knew she was huddled on the floor, with Carol leaning over her, her lovely face chalk-white with shock. 'My God,' Carol gasped. 'What happened?'

'It's all right,' Leaning against Carol's shoulder, Mia closed her eyes and waited for the world to stop spinning. 'It happens sometimes,' she breathed. 'Nothing to worry about. I'll be fine in a moment or two.'

'But you fainted!' Carol gasped. 'That can't be normal, can it?'

'It is for me,' Mia said, a trifle ruefully. 'If you could help me get to my feet, I think I would be better lying down in bed now.'

'Of course.' Eager to help, but feeling guilty for bringing on the faint, Carol helped Mia to her feet. Together they mounted the stairs.

In the bedroom Mia dropped weakly onto the bed and lay there with her eyes closed while Carol hovered anxiously, uncertain what to do next.

'Can I get you a drink or something?' she offered in the end.

'Mmm.' Mia nodded carefully. 'That would be nice. Just a glass of water, please.'

Two minutes later Carol was back with the water and Mia was able to sit up and drink it, without feeling dizzy. 'Mia...' Carol began cautiously. 'Please don't let Alex know what I said before,' she begged. 'He's always going on about my big mouth. If he finds out I've been baiting you with it my life isn't going to be worth living around here...'

Thinking about it now the anger had subsided, along with the dizziness, Mia supposed the other woman was right. What was the use in causing yet more friction in a situation that was already too full of it?

'If you don't tell him that I fainted just now,' she bargained. 'He knows it happens,' she quickly assured Carol at her immediate protest. 'But he'll stop me from visiting

Suzanna if he hears about it, and at the moment the little girl needs me.'

'OK,' Carol agreed, but she sounded reluctant, to say the least. 'I'll say nothing about you fainting if you'll not chuck him out of this room so he knows my mouth's been working overtime again. Deal?'

'Deal,' Mia agreed, then lay back again as the front door slammed and the sound of two male voices drifted up the stairs.

'I'll go and head him off,' Carol said, shifting quickly to the door. 'If he sees you looking this washed-out he'll know something's wrong with you.'

Then she was gone. Mia could hear their voices through the half-open door. 'Where's Mia?' Alex was demanding. 'Why is your bag lying on the floor with its contents tipped all over the place?'

'Mia is tired and has gone to bed,' Mia heard Carol answer. 'She said to tell you not to disturb her when you came up. And my bag is on the floor like that because I was so desperate for the loo when I got home that I just dropped it and ran. Any more questions?'

It was a challenge, and one issued with her usual flippancy that belied any hint of deceit. The voice changed and became the brother's, whose tones were warmer as he greeted his wife the way loving husbands did.

After that, all went quiet as the three of them disappeared into the kitchen and Mia dragged herself up, got herself undressed and into her nightdress then fell between the sheets.

She slept very heavily and woke the next morning feeling thick-headed and lethargic. By the imprint on the pillow beside her, Alex had shared her bed last night, though whether he'd stayed there all night or had spent half of it stretched out in the chair she didn't know or care.

She was still angry with him for discussing their private business with the rest of his family. It made her feel ex-

posed, more the outsider than ever, even though, on the
face of it, he had allowed her closer to his family here in
London than he had done while they were living in Greece.

When she went downstairs she found Carol alone in the
kitchen. The men had apparently already left for work, and
it was Carol who drove her to the hospital. Mia spent the
morning entertaining Suzanna, who was allowed out of bed
today and was walking around although she found it sore
to do so.

They had just finished lunch, and Suzanna was resting
on her bed while Mia read a story to her, when Alex walked
in. He sent Mia a fleeting glance and then directed his attention at Suzanna.

'You look much brighter today.' He smiled.

The child smiled, too, her face lighting up like a puppy
starved of affection who saw the chance of some coming
its way in the shape of this man.

'I've drawn you a picture,' she told Alex shyly, and
asked Mia to pass her a new sketch pad Carol had given
her yesterday. 'It's to say thank you for my computer
game...'

Inside were three pictures, although there was another
one, which Mia had already been given for herself, of a
church with a bride and bridegroom standing outside it and
a child standing beside them, her hand tucked in the
groom's. It said such a lot about the child's secret wishes
that Mia had had to fight the urge to weep when Suzanna
had handed the picture to her. Now she had it safely tucked
away in the carrier bag in which she had brought Suzanna's
gift—the set of story books they had just started reading.
One of the set, *The Lion, the Witch and the Wardrobe*, was
Suzanna's favourite story.

Now the child was solemnly handing Alex his picture. It
showed blue skies and a large sun, beaming down on a
man, a woman, a little girl and a baby around a swimming
pool with a pretty house in the background.

More secret wishes unwittingly portrayed for the discerning to read. Mia had told Suzanna all about Alex's villa on Skiathos, and she had drawn herself there with them because that was where she most wanted to be.

No, thought Mia, Alex was not a fool. The way his eyes were hooded as he studied the picture meant he was reading all the right messages.

'I have one for the other lady, too,' Suzanna told Alex shyly.

'Carol,' Mia said.

'Carol,' Suzanna obediently repeated. 'She brought me these felt tips and the sketch pad,' she explained to Alex. 'She wanted me to draw my operation so I have—do you think she'll like it?'

This picture was gory in the extreme. When Alex finally managed to drag his attention away from his own offering to look at Carol's picture, he couldn't help the rueful smile that touched his mouth. 'I should think she will love it.' he murmured very drily. 'Thank you for my picture.'

From being ready for a nap, Suzanna was suddenly so animated Mia felt something painful clutch at her heart as she watched the little girl hunt in the clutter on her bed to unearth her computer game, which she handed to Alex.

'Would you like to have a go?' she offered eagerly, switching it on for him. 'You press this button here, then—'

It was like watching a light go out. One moment all three of them seemed to be basking in the brilliance of Suzanna's excitement and in the next, darkness fell in the form of a metaphorical big black shadow. The child had glanced up, that was all—just glanced up distractedly—and, wham, she was a different person.

Mia was sitting on the side of the bed, with Alex seated in the chair on the other side. She looked up, too, and rose jerkily. Alex glanced up, saw who was standing in the doorway and frowned as his eyes flicked to the other two then back to the door again.

Jack Frazier was standing there, transfixed. His eyes were locked on Mia's body, greed glinting in their cold grey depths as he absorbed the obvious evidence of her pregnancy.

'So it is done,' he said with unmasked satisfaction. 'Why didn't you tell me?' The accusing words were flashed at Mia. 'When is it due?' He laughed, and turned to Alex, who was rising slowly to his feet. 'I can't damn well believe it! Well done, man. Well done!'

Not seeing or completely ignoring Alex's grim expression, Jack Frazier walked forward to grab his hand and began to pump it up and down.

'When do we close the deal, then?' he asked eagerly.

On the other side of the bed Mia was reaching for Suzanna's hand as the child's hand searched for hers. Neither smiled. Neither spoke. As far as Jack Frazier was concerned, they might as well not have been there for all they mattered. Mia only mattered as a vessel required to make him his so-called grandson and Suzanna didn't matter at all.

'We will let you know at the appropriate time,' Alex said coldly. 'As it is, Suzanna's health is the main concern in this room.'

As a pointed reminder of his duty, Jack took the hint and at last condescended to notice Suzanna. 'Got your Mia back, then?' he taunted drily. 'The lengths children will go to get their own way.'

'She didn't stage-manage appendicitis,' Mia said tightly, as the poor child lowered her head so she didn't have to look into those coldly indifferent eyes.

'No?' He sounded dubious. 'Well, never mind about that. I want to know about my grandson. Were you going to bother to tell me at all, or was I supposed to wait until the damned thing was over and done with before I found out anything?'

She didn't answer—she refused to. She had nothing whatsoever to say to him that he didn't already know.

'Like that, is it?' He grimaced. 'Well, at least you carried through. I did wonder with this long silence whether you'd chickened out at the last hurdle. But...' he glanced at Suzanna's lowered head again '...we all have our price, don't we, Mia? And your price almost became a non-runner. I wonder what you would have done then?'

It was such a cruel thing to suggest that Mia actually swayed in horror. Luckily, the child didn't understand what he was talking about—but Alex did. In one step he had hold of Jack Frazier's arm.

'Let's go for a walk,' he suggested grimly. 'We have a few things to say to each other, I think...'

He had them both out of the door before Mia could react. The dire threat in his words filled her with such a dark sense of impending horror that her legs went from beneath her. She slumped down beside Suzanna and pulled the little girl close to her breast.

He couldn't mean what she feared he'd meant, she told herself desperately. Alex wouldn't break a confidence and tell her father that he knew about Suzanna, would he?

Oh, please, she prayed as she held the little girl even closer. Please don't let him say anything stupid!

'Daddy hates me,' Suzanna whispered painfully.

'No, he doesn't, darling,' Mia said soothingly. 'He just doesn't know how to love anyone, that's all.'

It was the truth. Her father was incapable of loving anyone. The man was a single-minded egotist who measured his own strength in his ability to close his heart to others. He had done it with her mother, with his children and with all his competitors when he'd squeezed them dry without conscience. He saw himself as omnipotent, his only regret in life being the loss of his son to carry on his name even if he hadn't been his blood heir. To Jack Frazier that hadn't mattered so long as Tony bore his name.

Now he had to accept second best in a child who would bear the name of its father and not its grandfather, but it was written into the contract he had drawn up with Alex that the child Mia carried would be given the second name of Frazier. For Jack Frazier, that was going to be good enough for him to bequeath his millions.

He made her sick. The whole filthy situation made her sick! The sooner it was over the sooner she could begin to wash her life clean again.

Alex didn't come back. Mia spent the rest of the afternoon worrying about what he'd said to her father. By the time Carol arrived, with Leon in tow, she felt so tired and wretched she was more than ready to leave.

But Suzanna was still feeling the effects of Jack Frazier's visit, and at least Carol's bright chatter helped to lift the child's mood again. Leon was quiet but, then, he always was. He glanced often at Mia who had removed herself to the window and stood there, gazing out with a bleakness that isolated her from the rest of those present.

While Carol was sitting on the bed, drawing a bold picture in Suzanna's sketch book, Leon came over to stand beside Mia.

'Are you all right?' he asked quietly.

It surprised her enough to glance at him. 'Tired, that's all.' She tried a smile and almost made it happen before she was turning to stare out of the window again.

'Alex was coming back to get you himself, but something came up only he could deal with. He asked me to ask you if you would mind waiting until he gets in tonight before you retire because he has something important he wishes to discuss with you.'

Something to do with her father? Mia wondered fretfully, and gave a nod of acquiescence.

'Thank you.' Politely Leon moved away from her again. He didn't like her, Mia knew. He resented the pressure her father had used on his brother. He resented her presence in his brother's life.

Back at the house, Mia found enough energy from somewhere to help Carol prepare dinner, then sat and ate with them in the dining room, though she felt like an intruder. But it was either eat with them or go to her room and eat alone, which would have been rude in the extreme. By the time they had cleared away after the meal, and Alex still hadn't put in an appearance, Mia couldn't take the tension any longer and excused herself with an apology.

'I just can't keep awake any longer,' she explained. 'I'm so sorry.'

She had just climbed wearily into bed when the bedroom door opened. *Alex looks less than his usually immaculate self* was the first anxious thought to hit her. He needed a shave and his clothes looked decidedly the worse for wear. His hair was rumpled, as if he had been raking impatient fingers through it.

'I'm sorry I'm so late,' he said, when he saw she was awake, 'but this could not wait until the morning.'

He closed the door and continued to stand there for a few moments, his tired face brooding as he studied the pensive way she was sitting in bed, banked by snowy white pillows, waiting for him to say what he had to say.

Then he sighed—heavily. 'Look, do you mind if I take a quick shower before we talk?' he asked tiredly.

'N-no, of course not,' she replied, but she would have preferred him just to get on and say what he had to because she didn't like the grim mood he was in, and she needed to know what he had discussed with her father. But he had already walked off into the bathroom, leaving her sitting there trapped in an electric state of tension.

True to his word, though, he was back in minutes. He had showered and shaved and looked marginally less weary, though no less grim, wrapped in a blue towelling bathrobe that left too much naked golden flesh on show for her comfort because her imagination was suddenly conjuring up images that set her over-sensitive breasts tingling and made that place between her thighs begin to throb.

Her knees came up, her arms loosely wrapping around them in an instinctive act of defensive protection for those susceptible parts of her body. But her eyes never left him as he came over to the bed and sat down on it beside her, the tension seeming to sing loud in the quietness of the softly lit bedroom.

'What's wrong, Alex?' Mia asked anxiously, unable to hold the question back any longer.

His dark eyes flicked up and clashed with hers, then he smiled a rather rueful smile at her that did nothing for her equilibrium. 'Nothing,' he assured her, then went silent, those deceptively languid eyes of his studying her worried face for a few moments before he eventually went on, 'Nothing that you need worry about, anyway…'

He did a strange thing then. He reached up to touch her hair, gently combing it away from her cheek and one creamy shoulder. The electricity in the air sharpened, sprinkling that well-remembered static all around her. Her heart began to race, those two over-active parts of her body sending her another jolt that reminded her just how irresistible she found this man.

'I have to return to Greece,' he announced, making her blink and forcing her to come back from wherever she had flown off to—bringing reality tumbling back into perspective. 'I expect to be gone for about three weeks.'

His hand dropped away. She wanted to shiver, as if she'd just been shut out in the cold, and hated herself for being this vulnerable to him.

'I accept that you cannot leave Suzanna yet,' he continued while she struggled with her foolish emotions, 'so I have arranged with Carol and Leon for you to stay here for now.'

At least he wasn't making her return to Greece with him,

Mia noted with relief, although remaining under this roof with his brother so clearly resenting her presence didn't exactly fill her with joy. Still, she'd lived with worse, she told herself bracingly. And she could spend most of her time with Suzanna—keep herself as scarce around here as possible.

'The other problem is Suzanna,' he went on, as if his own train of thought was following the same lines as her own. 'She is due to be discharged from hospital in a couple of days.'

'I'll go with her to my father's house,' Mia offered instantly. 'It seems the best thing all round. I won't be putting anyone here out.'

Alex was already shaking his head. 'No,' he said. 'I will not have you exposed to your father in your condition so I have done a deal with him.'

Mia stiffened instantly. 'You didn't tell him you knew the truth about her, did you?' she asked tensely.

'Of course not!' he snapped. 'What do you take me for— a monster? You think I was blind to the way that child shrivelled up in his presence—the way you did the same thing yourself? You think I enjoy watching any child react to an adult like that?'

Mia lowered her lashes and said nothing—after all, it wasn't that long ago that he'd enjoyed seeing her cringe from him.

The air grew thick, laden with anger, then he sighed heavily. 'You cannot bring yourself to trust me even a small amount, can you?' he muttered. 'So, what do you suspect I am about to say to you now? That I have sold you into purdah for the duration of your pregnancy?'

'Why not?' she shot back. 'I was in purdah before we came to London. Why not put me back there again?'

'I have offered to take Suzanna off your father's hands for the next three weeks until she returns to her school,' he cut in tightly. 'Your father has agreed, so long as you both reside at this house and Suzanna is not taken out of the country!'

'He's agreed to that?' Mia couldn't believe it.

'He almost bit my damned hand off!' Alex rasped in disgust. 'Apparently, his housekeeper is about to take her annual vacation, which meant him having to hunt around for someone who could temporarily take charge of the child. So you being here fitted in very well with his own situation!'

'Oh,' she said, disconcerted by the amount of thought he had put into all of this. 'Thank you,' she mumbled belatedly.

'That is not all,' he continued, all that softness she had glimpsed in him a moment ago well and truly gone. 'I have my own provisos to add to your father's. The main one is that you promise me you will come back to Greece the day you take Suzanna back to school. The reason I demand this is because I will not be able to get back to London to collect you myself so I am going to have to take your word for it that you will come back to me.'

'I'll come back,' she promised, frowning because she had never so much as considered doing anything else. They had made a deal, one where she had agreed to give birth to his son on Greek soil. 'I will drive Suzanna back to school, then catch the next scheduled flight to—'

'My plane will be waiting for you at an airfield close to Suzanna's school,' he interrupted. 'And you will not drive yourself anywhere while you are here,' he went on grimly. 'One of my own drivers will be left at your disposal for the rest of your stay here.'

'But I have a car!' she protested. 'It's sitting, doing nothing, at my father's house! It would be nice to drive myself again while I'm here in London!'

'Not while you keep fainting,' he said.

'I do not keep fainting!' She hotly denied that.

'But those dizzy spells affect you too readily for you to

be safe behind the wheel of a car. I saw the way you barely managed to hold yourself upright in front of your father at lunchtime,' he added tightly when she opened her mouth to protest yet again. 'So you agree to my terms or I take you back to Greece with me now. The choice is yours.'

He was, after all, only protecting his investment! 'Yes, oh, master,' she said sarcastically.

He had been about to stand up when she'd said that, but now he stilled and Mia felt a frisson of warning shoot down her spine as he turned those dark eyes on her—she recognised the look, recognised it only too well.

'You know…' he said, super-light, super-soft, 'you are in real danger of baiting me once too often, *agape mou*. And, despite the delicacy of your condition or the fragility of that protective shell you like to hide behind, I am going to retaliate,' he warned her. 'And you're not going to like it because I know your secret.'

'I d-don't know what you're talking about,' she said warily.

'No?' he said quizzically—and his dark face was suddenly very close to her face. Her eyelashes began to quiver, and her fingers clutched nervously at the sheet. 'Well, let us see, shall we?' he suggested silkily, and his mouth covered her trembling one.

It was like being tossed into a burning furnace—she caught fire that quickly. Her mind caught fire, as well as her body, and she wasn't even aware of how spectacularly she had done it until he was having to use force to prise her clinging fingers from his nape before he could separate his mouth from her greedily clinging one.

'Now that…' he drawled, touching a punctuating fingertip to the pulsing fullness of her lips, 'is your secret. You may prefer to hate me, but you cannot damned well resist me!'

His words made her want to hit out at him, but he caught

the hand before it landed its blow and arrogantly pressed his warm lips to her palm.

That was the point where her sense of humiliation plumbed new depths because the moment she felt his tongue make a salacious lick of her palm she was lost again. Her eyes closed and her breathing ruptured as that lick sent its sensual message down her arm and through her body, arrowing directly at the very core of her.

'I can delay my departure for an hour or two, if you want me to...' he offered.

That stung a different part of her entirely. Her eyes opened, angry fire burning alongside the passion. 'Only an hour or two?' she said scathingly. 'Well, that just about puts your attitude to sex in a nutshell, doesn't it? One quick fix then you're off again before the sheets get warm!'

He should have been angry—she'd said it all to make him so angry that he would walk out! But he completely disconcerted her by arrogantly taking up the challenge.

'You want more than that? A whole night of wild passion, maybe?'

'You aren't capable of spending a whole night in the same bed as me!' she said scornfully.

His eyes darkened. Mia felt real alarm take a stinging dive down the length of her spine. 'That lousy opinion you have of me really does need amending,' he said curtly. Suddenly he was standing up, determined fingers already working on the knot to his robe.

'W-what are you doing?' she choked. 'No, Alex...' she protested huskily, not even trying to pretend that she didn't know exactly why he was stripping himself.

It didn't stop him. Her heart began to race, her tongue cleaving itself to the roof of her dry mouth as she watched in a paralysed mix of greedy fascination and mind-numbing horror that magnificent naked frame of his appear in front of her.

The air left her lungs on a short, sharp gasp at the un-

ashamed power of his pulsing arousal. Her eyes moved upwards to clash with the fierce flame in his as he bent to lift
the edge of the sheet.

At last she found the motivation to attempt an escape,
slithering like a snake to the other side of the bed. His arm
caught her before she could get away. It drew her back
across the smooth white linen, then turned her so she was
facing him.

'I'm pregnant,' she reminded him shakily, as if that
should be enough to stop him.

It wasn't. His arm slid beneath her shoulders then angled
downwards across her spine so his hand could arch her
slender hips towards him. The firm roundness of her stomach was pressed into the concaved wall of his taut stomach.
He sighed a little unsteadily, his darkened eyes closing as
if this first physical contact he was having with their unborn
child was moving him deeply.

Enthralled by his totally unexpected reaction, Mia released a soft gasp. He heard it—felt the warm rush of air
brush across his face—and opened eyes which had gone
pitch black and seemed to want to draw her deep inside
them.

Which is exactly what he did do. He didn't speak—he
didn't need to. That expression had said it all for him. It
was need. It was desire. It was hunger too long-standing
for him to fight it any longer.

The last conscious thought she had before he completely
took her over was that he'd been right. She can't resist him,
not when he looked at her like that, anyway.

Her eyes began to close, her soft mouth parting as it went
in blind search of his. They fused from mouth to breast to
hip. It was that easy to give in to it in the end.

For the next few hours they became lost in each other,
the world outside with all its complications shut right out.

'Why?' Mia asked a long time later when they were lying

in a heated tangle of sensually exhausted limbs. 'When you rejected me the first night we came here.'

'I promised you I would not touch you again once you were pregnant,' he replied.

'You made that promise to yourself, Alex,' Mia corrected him quietly. 'I never asked you for it.'

He was silent for a moment, then gave a small sigh. 'Well, it is now a broken promise,' he announced, 'and one I have no intention of reinstating.'

Then he kissed her again, slowly, languidly, drawing her back down into that deep, dark well of pleasure from where she eventually drifted into a sated sleep, her arms still holding him and his still wrapped around her. It felt wonderful—so different from anything they had shared before that it was like a statement of future intent.

Yet when she awoke the next morning he was gone—as usual.

Which meant—what? she wondered grimly. A return to the status quo, with the sex thrown back in to spice it all up a bit?

CHAPTER NINE

SUZANNA was discharged from hospital three days later, and the time that followed went by much too quickly. Time that turned out to be a lot pleasanter than Mia had expected it to be, mainly because Leon's manner towards her had softened remarkably—though forced to do so, she suspected, by a child who was so very eager to please that even Leon Doumas didn't seem to have the heart to be anything but pleasant around Suzanna.

And that meant he had to include Mia.

Everywhere the little girl went, her fluffy rabbit, her pens and paper and her computer game went with her. Every night she insisted Mia read a story from her set of books. When in their company, her wistful green eyes followed Leon and Carol around like a love-starved puppy, eagerly waiting to be noticed. When not in their company she talked about them constantly, starry-eyed and happy, so pathetically grateful to the couple for allowing her to come and stay with them that sometimes it brought tears to Mia's eyes to witness it.

With the resilience of childhood she recovered quickly from her operation, and with the vulnerability of childhood she worried constantly about the moment when she would have to go back to school because she knew that was also the time when Mia would be going back to Greece.

'You might forget all about me when you have the new baby to love,' she confided one evening as she lay in the bed Carol had allocated her in the room next to Mia's.

'New babies don't steal love from one person for themselves, darling,' Mia said gently. 'They only ask that you

let them share it. Do you think you can do that? Share all
the love I have for you with this new baby?'

'Will Alex let me come and visit sometimes, do you
think?' she asked anxiously. 'Will he mind if I share you
with the new baby?'

'Of course not,' Mia said. 'Who was it who convinced
Daddy to let you come and stay here until you go back to
school?'

'Carol said Alex likes children,' the child said, with that
painfully familiar wistful expression. 'She said Alex likes
me because I look so much like you.'

Well, that was a very kind thing to say, Mia acknowledged, and made a mental note to thank Carol when she
next saw her.

Carol just shrugged her thanks aside. 'It was only the
truth,' she said. 'Alex does like children and he's got himself so tied up in knots over you that he's bound to like
Suzanna simply because she looks like you.'

Tied up in what kind of knots? she wondered. Sexual
knots? 'You don't know what you're talking about,' she
replied dismissively.

'No?' To her annoyance, Carol started grinning. 'Did
Alex ever tell you about his mistress?' she asked. When
Mia instantly stiffened up Carol nodded, 'I thought he
would. I know how his mind works, you see, and he would
have told you about her just to score points off you. But I
bet he hasn't told you that within a week of marrying you
he had sent her packing.

'No,' Carol continued drily at Mia's start of surprise, 'I
didn't think he would. Too bad for his ego to admit that,
having had you, he couldn't bring himself to touch another
woman. But that's our dear Alex for you,' she went on.
'Committed. Totally committed to whatever he turns his
attention to.'

'Like an island he wants to repossess,' Mia said derisively, refusing to believe a word Carol was saying because

believing would make her start seeing Alex through different eyes, which in turn could make her weak.

And she couldn't afford to be weak where Alex was concerned. She was already vulnerable enough.

'Certainly, recovering the family island has been the goal that has driven him for the past ten years,' Carol agreed. 'But marry some strange woman and produce a child with her in the quest for that goal?' She shook her blonde head. 'Now that was going too far, even for Alex. Or so I thought,' she added sagely, 'until I met you. Then I began to wonder if half the trap wasn't of his own making.'

'It wasn't,' Mia said coolly. 'My father is a master tactician.' And then some, she added bitterly to herself.

'Your father knew why Alex wanted the island back so badly,' Carol acknowledged. 'A solemn promise to his dying father—you can't really get a bigger incentive than that for a Greek. But I still say—'

'His father?' Mia cut in sharply. 'Alex promised his dying father?'

'Didn't you know?' Carol looked surprised. 'Come on,' she said suddenly, taking hold of Mia's hand as she did so. 'It will be easier to show you,' she explained, pulling Mia into the hall and then into a room Carol used as a working studio. 'See,' she declared, bringing Mia to a halt in front of a large framed painting.

It was titled *Vision* and Mia's heart stilled as she recognised it as the original of the print she had seen in the lift at the Doumas office building.

'Their father had this painted when he knew he was going to have to sell the island,' Carol explained. 'Until then it had been in the family for ever. See the little graveyard.' She pointed it out. 'Every Doumas, except their father, is buried there, including their mother and their older brother. They were killed in a flying accident when Alex was a teenager and Leon a small child. The accident devastated their father. He adored his wife and worshipped his eldest son.

'With them gone, he felt he had nothing left to live for, hence the sudden drop in the Doumas fortunes. His own health suffered until he eventually died prematurely—but not before he had extracted a promise from Alex that he would get the island back and have his remains transferred there. Do you understand now?' she demanded finally.

'Understand?' Mia repeated. Oh, yes, she acknowledged heavily, she understood. Alex's island in the Aegean was not just a piece of rock for which he was willing to sell his soul. It was home. It was where his heart lay, right there with his mother and his brother and where his father needed to lay his own heart.

She finally did understand that the grip her own father had on Alex was easily as tight as the grip he had on herself. Blackmail—emotional blackmail. A far more powerful vice than mere financial blackmail.

Her hand came up to cover her mouth. 'I'm going to be sick,' she choked, and had to run to the nearest cloakroom.

It was ironic, really, that Alex should choose to call her that same evening. 'Are you all right?' he demanded the moment she announced herself on the phone. 'Carol said you were sick earlier.'

'Something I ate. I'm fine now,' she said dismissively, hoping Carol hadn't told him exactly why she had been sick.

And what had made her sick? Her own words coming back to haunt her. Cruel words, dreadful words, where she'd condemned him for selling himself for physical gain while she'd self-righteously seen herself as selling herself for love.

'You must not overdo it now that Suzanna is out of hospital,' he commanded rather curtly.

'I won't,' she said. 'She's quite an easy child to entertain.'

'I noticed,' he muttered. 'Too damned easy to please. Have you seen your father?'

Mia frowned at his sharpened tone. 'No,' she replied.

'Good,' Alex grunted. 'Let us hope it stays that way.'

'Is that why you're calling?' she asked. It was so unusual for him to bother. 'Because you're concerned about my father showing up here? He won't, you know,' she assured him. 'Having reassured himself that all is going to plan, he won't waste thinking time on me again until the baby is due.'

'Does that bother you?'

Bother me? Again she frowned at the strangely sharp question. 'No,' she said firmly. Her father's lack of interest in her as a person had stopped hurting her a long time ago.

'Good,' he said again. 'I have two reasons for calling you,' he went on, suddenly becoming all brisk and businesslike. 'You are due your monthly check-up with the doctor this week. Since it is not logical to transport you to Athens for a simple doctor's appointment, I have therefore arranged an appointment at a clinic in London for you.'

He went on to give her names, addresses, dates and times which she had to hurriedly write down.

'And the other reason I called,' he continued, 'is because I have just discovered that I have your passport here in Athens with me. I must have stashed it in my briefcase without thinking about it, when we travelled to London, and there it has stayed until I unearthed it this morning. I also happened to notice that it still bears your maiden name, which makes it invalid.'

'Oh,' she said. She hadn't given a single thought to either her passport or the fact that it was no longer valid. 'I suppose that means I will have to apply for a new one.'

'I am already arranging it,' he announced. 'Leon is seeing to the paperwork so we can get it rushed through before you leave for Greece. You will need to put your signature to the forms Leon is preparing and supply a new photograph. Can you see to that first thing in the morning?'

'Of course,' she said, 'but I could just as easily have seen to the rest as well. I'm pregnant, not an invalid, you know!'

'I never meant to imply you were.' He sighed. 'But I presumed you would prefer to devote your time in England to Suzanna,' he said, in a tone meant to remind her exactly where her priorities lay.

Which it did—irksomely. 'Is that it?' she said, sounding childishly uncivil even to her own ears.

She heard him mutter something that sounded very much like a profanity. 'Why do you have to turn every conversation into a battle?' he said wearily.

'Why do you have to be so damned arrogant?' she shot back, for want of something to toss at him.

'Because I'm trying to save you a lot of unnecessary hassle.'

'I don't like my life being organised for me!' she snapped.

'I am trying to help you, damn it!' he exploded. 'When are you going to stop being so damned bitter and realise that I am your ally, not your enemy!'

When you stop tying my emotions in so many knots that I just can't tell what you are any more! she thought wretchedly, and slammed down the phone before she actually yelled the words at him!

Then she stood, shaken to the very roots by her own anger, because she didn't know what she was angry about!

Yes, you do, a little voice inside her head told her. You want him to show you a little care and consideration, but when he does you get so frightened it isn't real that you simply go off the deep end!

Leon produced the relevant forms for her to sign the next evening—several of them, which made her frown.

'Copies in case I mess up,' he explained dismissively.

She shrugged and signed where he told her to sign, and handed over the requested photographs—four surprisingly good snaps, taken in a passport booth in the local high street. Carol had gone with her and so had Suzanna, and between them they had turned the excursion into a game.

Mia now had in her possession several photos of Suzanna pulling silly faces into the camera, and even a couple of Carol, doing the same thing.

She kept her appointment at the exclusive London clinic Alex had arranged for her. They gave her the full works, blood pressure, blood tests, physical examination and an ultrasound scan. No problems anywhere, she was relieved to hear. The dizzy spells were a sign of low blood sugar levels, easily remedied by keeping light snacks handy. Other than that, she was assured, they were nothing to worry about. She left the clinic feeling very relieved to have a clean bill of health—and a black and white photograph of her darling baby curled up inside her womb.

'Did it hurt?' Carol asked suspiciously as she studied the picture.

'What, the scan?' Mia asked. 'No,' she said. 'It just feels a bit strange, that's all—and they did prod and poke the poor thing a bit until they could get him to lie in a good position.'

Carol handed back the photograph, but there was an odd look in her eyes that Mia couldn't interpret—a look that bothered her for days afterwards, though she didn't know why.

Another week went by, and Alex didn't call again—not that she expected him to after the last row they'd had. But it hurt in some ways that he hadn't even bothered to call to see how her visit to the clinic had gone—though she would rather die that let him know that.

Then other, far more immediate concerns began to take precedence, not least the way Suzanna grew quieter and more withdrawn as their three weeks raced towards their imminent conclusion.

Carol found Mia one evening, weeping over Suzanna's school trunk which Mrs Leyton had had sent over to the house that day.

'Oh, Mia.' Carol sighed, and knelt to put her arms around her. 'Don't do this to yourself,' she murmured painfully.

'I can't bear to leave her,' Mia confided wretchedly. 'I don't know how I'm going to do it! She hates that school!' she sobbed. 'She hates being away from me! It's going to break her poor little heart and it's going to break mine, too!'

'Oh, dear God,' Carol groaned thickly. 'I can't cope with this. Mia, listen to me!' she pleaded. 'You—'

'Carol…'

It was the flatness in Leon's tone that stopped Carol from saying whatever she'd been about to say.

'Don't meddle,' he warned.

'But, Leon!' Carol cried. 'If Alex knew how—'

'I said, don't meddle,' he repeated.

He was standing in the open doorway to Mia's bedroom, and he sounded so formidable that when Mia glanced at him through tear-washed eyes she thought she could see Alex standing there. Alex, grim with resolve.

She shivered. They had a bargain, she and Alex, she reminded herself staunchly. A bargain that was too important to both of them for her to stumble at one of the very last hurdles.

'It's all right,' she said, pulling herself together so that by the time she had pulled herself to her feet all that cool dignity she had used to bring her this far was firmly back in place. 'I'm all right now.' She smiled a brittle smile at the tearful Carol as she also straightened. 'But thank you for caring.'

'We all care, Mia,' Carol murmured anxiously. 'Though I can well understand why you wouldn't believe that.'

The next day Suzanna's trunk left for the school by spe-

cial carrier. The morning after that, pale but composed—
they'd both been through this many times before, after all—
Mia and Suzanna came down the stairs together, the child
dressed in her dour black and grey school uniform and Mia
in a sober grey long-jacketed suit, prim high-collared white
blouse and with her hair neatly contained in a rather aus-
tere, if elegant, French pleat.

She expected to find Alex's chauffeur waiting for them,
but she had not expected to see both Leon and Carol standing there also.

'We're coming with you,' Carol explained. 'Alex's orders.'

Alex's orders. She almost smiled at the phrase, only she
couldn't smile.

The journey to Bedfordshire was utterly harrowing.
Suzanna sat between Mia and Carol in the back of the car
while Leon took the front seat next to the driver.

One of the little girl's hands was locked in Mia's and,
clicking into a sort of autopilot, Mia talked softly to the
child as they swept out of London onto the motorway and
kept on talking as the car ate up the miles far too quickly.

As they left the motorway Suzanna began to recognise
her surroundings and grew tense, her hand clinging all the
tighter to Mia's. A couple of miles away from the school
entrance the tears began to threaten. Carol muttered something very constricted, then reached out jerkily to grab at
Suzanna's other hand.

'Hey,' she said, with very forced lightness, 'this is an
adventure for me. I've never been this way before!'

'I hate it,' Suzanna whispered.

'But look!' Carol urged. 'There's a private airfield over
there! I can see a beautiful white plane sitting on the tar-
mac.'

Airfield.

Mia shivered. It ran through her like a dousing from an
ice-cold shower.

'You know,' Carol was saying brightly, 'Alex has a plane just like that one! Do you think he may have come to—?'

'What's going on?' Mia interrupted sharply as the car suddenly took a *sharp* right turn. She leaned forward, staring out of the car window. 'Why have we turned here?' she demanded.

To her confusion, Carol chuckled. 'A magical mystery tour,' she chanted excitedly.

The car stopped. Mia stared and her heart began to pound heavily in her chest for in front of them, just as Carol had indicated, stood a gleaming white Gulfstream jet, with its engines running.

'No,' she breathed. 'No!' she gasped more strongly as a horrified suspicion of what was actually happening here began to take a firm hold on her. 'Carol, this is—!'

But Carol was already clambering out of the car—and taking Suzanna with her!

'Leon!' Mia entreated jerkily.

'Trust us,' he said, then climbed out of the car—and that was when panic suddenly erupted.

'You can't do this!' she protested, scrambling out of the car in time to see Carol and Suzanna disappear onto the jet. 'No!' she shouted after them. 'Oh, God!' Leon's arm came round her shoulders. 'Leon, for the love of God, you don't understand!'

'Believe me,' he said soothingly, 'I do understand. It's OK…' He began urging her towards the plane. 'Alex has fixed everything. You have no need to worry. Trust him, Mia. He has your best interests at heart…'

Best interests at heart? Her blood pressure began to rise in a swirling red mist that almost completely engulfed her. She stumbled up the steps, dangerously out of control and near collapse. With her eyes she frantically searched out and found Suzanna—then saw the man who was squatting next to the child, talking to her.

'Alex,' she gasped in confusion.

His dark head came up, his eyes giving her a look of such grim determination that any small threads of pretence she might have been clinging to that this was not what she feared it was snapped at that moment.

As if in rehearsed confirmation, Suzanna's voice reached out towards her, shrill with rising excitement. 'I'm coming to Greece to live with you, Mia! I don't have to go back to that horrid school!'

'No,' she breathed in pulse-drumming horror. 'Alex, you just can't do this!'

'Go and sit next to Carol and fasten yourself in, Suzanna,' Alex urged the ecstatic child.

He straightened, lean and lithe and dauntingly real in a casually loose taupe linen jacket, black trousers and a black T-shirt that did nothing to disguise the tight contours of his body as he began striding towards her. Even in the midst of all this trauma Mia found herself in a tense state of suspended animation, her senses remembering the man's sensual might and not the might of his ruthless intellect.

'Be calm,' he was murmuring soothingly. 'There is no need to panic...'

No need to panic. The words rattled frantically around her. No need to panic? Of course there was a need to panic! This was wrong! This was crazy! It was going to ruin everything!

Behind her she heard the muffled thud of the plane's outer door sealing into its housing and the jet engines give a threatening roar. Her whole body quivered in violent reaction, the clammy heat of horror suddenly racing through her blood, and on a whimpering groan of pained accusation aimed at those compelling dark eyes that were coming ever closer she pitched dizzyingly forward into total oblivion.

She came round to find herself stretched out across two soft leather chairs, with a pillow tucked beneath her head and Alex squatting beside her, his fingers impatiently dealing with the tiny pearl buttons that held her blouse collar fastened at her throat.

He looked pale, grim-faced and extremely angry. 'I swear to God, with everything I have in me,' he railed at her the moment he saw her eyes flutter open, 'that you will spend the rest of this pregnancy locked away in a bloody stress-free environment!'

The blouse button sprang free. He sat back on his heels, his eyes flashing with rage when he saw her catch in a greedy breath of air.

'And the power dressing gets its walking orders as well!'

Still too dizzy to fight back, Mia lifted an arm to her face so she could cover her aching eyes with decidedly icy fingers. Almost instantly, the hand snapped away from her eyes again. They were already in the air! She could hear the aircraft's engines as nothing more than a faint purr as they flew them ever further away from England!

Shakily she pushed herself into a weak-limbed sitting position, her green eyes flicking urgently around the plush cream interior of the cabin.

They were alone. 'Where's Suzanna?' she demanded jerkily.

'In the galley with Carol, having the time of her life,' Alex said sardonically. 'We told her you were sleeping. She didn't see you swoon into my arms so she believed us.'

Is that what I did? Swooned right into the arms of the enemy?

So, what's new? she grimly mocked herself. You've been swooning into those arms from the very beginning! Knowing he was the enemy has never made any difference.

'Is anything else too tight on you?' Alex asked. His hands were already pushing the grey jacket down her arms.

'Will you stop doing that?' she snapped, trying to slap his hands away.

But the jacket came off, and his grim face did not unclench from the tension locking it as he angrily tossed the jacket away. Then he seemed to make a concerted effort to get a hold on his temper. A deep sigh ripped from him, his big shoulders flexed...

'I'm sorry about the cloak and dagger stuff,' he said heavily. 'I did not intend to frighten you so badly with it. I was afraid that if I had told you what I was going to do you would have panicked and warned your father.'

Which she would have done—Mia freely acknowledged that. 'But why, Alex?' she cried. 'Why are you doing this when you must know it will be Suzanna and me my father is going to punish for this bit of senseless defiance!'

'No defiance,' he said, shifting his long, lean frame into the chair directly opposite her own, where he leaned forward, placed his forearms on his spread knees and then, with the grimly controlled expression of a man who was about to drop a bombshell on the heads of the innocent, he announced impassively, 'I am calling the deal off.'

Mia just sat there, her blank, staring eyes telling him that she had not taken in what he was saying. He remained silent, waiting, watchful, noting the way her lips parted to aid the very frail thread of her breathing and the way her pale skin went even paler, the green of her eyes beginning to darken as the full import of his words finally began to sink in.

Her reaction, when it came, was not what he was expecting. 'Our deal?' she whispered tragically.

'No.' He frowned and shook his head. 'That is a completely separate issue, which I am not prepared to deal with right now. I am talking about my deal with your father. I am calling it off and, because I know that my decision is going to have a direct effect on you, I am placing both you and Suzanna under my protection. Which is why we are flying to Greece.'

'Protection?' she repeated. He was placing them under his protection when the very act of how he was doing it was effectively removing the only form of protection they had! 'How can you say that?' she cried. 'Legally, Suzanna is still his daughter! Legally, he can take her back whenever he wants to!'

'You *wanted* to leave her behind?' he challenged. 'You *wanted* to dump her at that school and walk away?'

No. 'But that's not the point,' she said with a sigh. 'My father—'

'Can do what the hell he likes,' Alex cut in grimly, throwing himself back in his seat in an act of indifference. 'But he will have to do it through legal channels because it is the only way he will get to see either of you again!'

Mia gasped, her mind burning up in horror at his cavalier attitude. 'But, Alex—this is abduction!' She pleaded with him to see the full import of what he was doing. 'You could be arrested for it! You could go to prison!'

'Try having a little faith,' he said.

Faith in what? she wondered deliriously. In him? In what he was doing? 'Suzanna doesn't even have a passport!' she told him shrilly.

His expression didn't alter by so much as a flicker as he reached into his jacket pocket and came out with something he tossed casually onto her lap.

Two passports. Two new British passports. Her stomach began to quiver, her icy fingers trembling as she made herself open both of them. She stared down at the two similar faces, which were staring right back at her.

One was an adult, the other a miniature version of that adult.

'H-how did you get this?' she whispered, picking up Suzanna's very own passport.

'With careful planning,' he replied drily.

'But...' Her eyes flickered downwards again, looking at the photograph of her daughter which was a match to the several sets she had tucked away in her bag.

Carol.

The full duplicity of what had been going on around her

for the last weeks finally hit her. 'You've all been very busy, it seems,' she managed to say at last.

'I am, by nature, very thorough,' Alex casually attested.

'Even to the point of getting my father's written permission for this?' she mocked,

'You authorised it.'

'What?' She stared at him blankly—only her eyes didn't remain blank because they were suddenly seeing that blur of forms Leon had got her to sign. 'Copies,' he'd called them, 'in case I mess up.'

'We will *all* end up in prison!' she said wretchedly.

To her absolute fury, he started to grin at her! Mia wanted to hit him! He never smiled at her—*never!* Yet he chose to do it now, in this dire situation.

'Oh, stop fretting,' he told her, leaning forward to take the two passports back and replace them in his jacket pocket before she had a chance to stop him. 'No one is going to question your connection with Suzanna when she looks so much like you!'

'It's still wrong, Alex!' she flashed back at him. 'And why go to all of this trouble, anyway?' she cried. 'It would all have been sorted out above board in a couple of months!'

To her utter confusion, his face closed up. 'I am not prepared to deal with that question at this present moment,' he said abruptly, and got up, his whole demeanour so grimly inflexible that she panicked.

'But, Alex!' she choked, jumping up to grab hold of his sleeve as he went to walk away from her. 'I need you to deal with it right now!'

'No,' he said, shook his arm free from her grasp then grimly walked away.

The rest of the long flight was achieved in an atmosphere of severely suppressed tension—suppressed because Suzanna was so clearly delighted with the whole wretched business that it would have been cruel to spoil it for her.

But it wasn't easy, and Mia retreated behind a cloak of cool repudiation where no one could reach her, except Suzanna.

They landed in Skiathos in the full heat of mid-afternoon, and Mia broke out in a cold sweat which didn't leave her until they were safely off the airport confines and driving away.

At every turn she had been expecting to see a group of officials bearing down on them to detain them—by order of her father.

But—no. She found herself safely ensconced in the passenger seat of the silver Mercedes, with Alex behind the wheel and Leon and Carol crushed into the back seat, with an excited Suzanna sitting between them.

The child chatted and bounced and asked question after question that, thankfully, the others answered because Mia couldn't lift her mood to fit the little girl's.

She felt shut off, bricked in behind a wall of anger, stress and a terrible sense of betrayal. She had begun to let herself like these people—to trust them even, which was no mean feat for someone who had learned a long time ago that trusting anyone was a terrible weakness.

Suzanna trusted them—Mia's eyes began to water. Suzanna was opening up like a blossoming flower to the warmth of their affection!

The car turned in through familiar gates and swept down the driveway to pull to a halt outside the front veranda.

Car doors opened, and they all climbed out. The sun was hot, the sea was blue and the white-painted walls of the house stood framed by the dense greens of the hillside behind.

'Is this going to be my new home?' Suzanna trilled in breathless wonder. 'Is it truly—is it?'

Mia spun to face Alex across the gleaming bonnet of the Mercedes. 'If you hurt her with this, I will never forgive you!' she said thickly, then turned to run into the house.

CHAPTER TEN

ALEX caught Mia in the hall, one hand curling around her slender wrist while the other clamped itself to her waist.

'Let go of me!' she protested.

His grip only tightened as he guided her—almost frog-marched her—up the stairs and into her bedroom. The door shut with the aid of his foot. Then he was tugging her round until she was facing him, his arms anchoring her there while she glared through a mist of bright, angry tears into his set face.

'I am *not* going to let anyone hurt Suzanna!' he blasted at her furiously. 'I am *not* doing this to hurt you!'

'Then why are you doing it?' she spat right back at him.

'I told you!' he rasped. 'I am pulling out of my deal with your father!'

'But *why?*' she repeated. 'Why, Alex, why?'

He let out a string of rasping profanities, frustration and anger blazing out of his eyes. 'Because of this!' he muttered, and caught her mouth with a kiss that knocked her senseless.

When he eventually let her up again for air she could barely stand up straight.

'I want you, I want our child and I want Suzanna *more* than I want my island!' he growled fiercely. 'Does that answer your question?'

Answer it? It virtually consumed it! He wanted her, really wanted her that badly?

Her face went white, her eyelashes flickering as she started to tremble. Her deeply inbred sense of caution stopped her from believing what he was actually trying to tell her. What his eyes were telling her as they blazed passionately down at her. What her own senses were pleading with her to believe!

'Don't faint on me!' she heard him mutter, and suddenly she was being lifted into his arms. 'Why is it,' he rasped as he strode towards the bed, 'that you either pass out or take my head off whenever I try to hold a meaningful conversation with you!'

He sat her down on the edge of the bed.

'You are driving me out of my mind!' he growled, coming down on his haunches in front of her. 'I cannot get close to you unless I use sex as a damned weapon!' he ranted. 'I cannot talk to you without feeling as if I am walking through a minefield of mistrust! And if I actually do manage to get through to you, you do this!'

'I'm not doing anything,' she whispered.

'You are trembling all over!' He harshly discarded her assurance.

'That's because you're shouting.'

'I'm not— Damn,' he grunted, as he caught himself shouting out a denial.

He sighed, lowered his head to run impatient fingers through his silky black hair, then sprang abruptly to his feet and moved right away from her over to one of the windows. He stood there with his hands thrust into his trouser pockets while he stared grimly outside, as if he needed time to recover his unexpected loss of composure.

'I want you to understand,' he muttered suddenly, 'that I have done what I have done because I needed to be sure that you and Suzanna were safe before I made a move on your father.'

'But why bother going to all this trouble at all?' she asked, still none the wiser as to why this had all been necessary. 'In a couple of months we could have had everything! You—your island, me—Suzanna, and my father his precious grandson!'

'No.' He refuted her words.

'Yes!' she insisted, coming to her feet on shaky legs that did not want to support her. 'Deciding to renege on your side of the deal now is not going to change the fact that I am pregnant with your son, Alex—which is all my father ever wanted anyway!'

'No, you're not.'

Mia blinked. 'I'm not what?' she demanded, her bewildered eyes fixing on the bunched muscles of his back.

The big shoulders flexed, his expression when he slowly turned to face her so sombre that she was arming herself for a really bad shock even before she knew she was doing it.

'You are not carrying my son.' He spelled it out more clearly.

'I beg your pardon?' Mia choked, then released a shaky laugh. 'What do you think this is, Alex?' she said mockingly, indicating her swollen abdomen. 'A mirage?'

'It's my daughter,' he replied.

'What?'

'Sit down again!' he barked at her when the colour drained out of her face, his long legs bringing him back to her side so he could push her back on the bed. 'My God,' he breathed harshly, 'I never would have thought such a strong-willed and fiery woman could be this physically frail!'

'I'm not frail,' she said in a broken whisper. 'I'm just shocked that you could say such a thing!'

'It is the truth.' He sighed. 'The scan you had last week shows no male genitalia—'

'But...' She was frowning in utter bemusement. 'Your family only makes male babies!'

'Not this time, it seems.' He grimaced.

'No.' She shook her head. 'I d-don't believe you. You weren't even there to see the scan!'

'Your doctor faxed a photocopy to me.'

He did? She blinked up at him, surprised to learn that

Alex had taken that much interest in her pregnancy. Then she remembered that she had her own copy of that scan, and she was as sure as she could be that it had not given any indication *what* sex their baby was!

She began glancing around her urgently, looking for her bag so she could check for herself what Alex was claiming.

He beat her to it, by gently placing his own small black and white print into her shaking fingers. After that she didn't move— not a muscle or even an eyelash. This photocopy of her scan was different from her own copy. Her baby had moved—and was showing clearly that Alex was telling the truth.

'Oh, heavens,' she gasped. 'How did that happen?'

It was a stupid question in anyone's books, and he said sardonically, 'By the usual methods, I should imagine.' The comment was probably well deserved—except Mia was in no fit state to appreciate it.

It was all suddenly becoming so wretchedly clear to her. What he'd gambled and what he'd lost. What he'd ended up being saddled with when he hadn't wanted any of it in the first place!

'Oh, Alex,' she breathed. 'I'm so very sorry!'

'Why should you apologise?' he drawled. 'We both know who takes responsibility for the sex of any child.'

'But your precious island!' She was barely listening to him.

Suddenly he was squatting in front of her again. 'Do I look like a man in need of sympathy?' he demanded. 'Look at me, Mia,' he insisted, when she kept her burning eyes lowered to that damning picture, then made her look at him by placing a gentle hand under her chin and lifting it.

His eyes weren't smiling exactly, but they were not miserable either. And his mouth was relaxed—a bit rueful maybe, and incredibly—

She sucked in a sharp gulp of air, shocked as to where

her mind had suddenly shot off to—and at such a calami-
tous moment like this!

'I have to confess to being rather pleased to be the first
Doumas to father a daughter in over a hundred years,' he
admitted sheepishly. 'I am also pleased,' he added more
soberly, 'that this unexpected development has saved me
from having to find another way of getting your father out
of all our lives.'

'He's not out of mine and Suzanna's yet,' Mia shakily
reminded him.

'But he will be,' Alex pledged.

'He's going to come after her, you know.'

'I want him to.' He nodded gravely, then raised his hands
to her trembling shoulders. 'Trust me,' he urged. 'Suzanna
is safe here. He cannot touch her. I know this absolutely,'
he declared. 'and by the time he arrives here I will be in a
situation to make *him* know it also!'

Mia wished she could be so sure about that. She knew
her father, knew how he responded to insubordination of
any kind. She shuddered.

Outside, a sound drifted up from the garden. It was the
laughter of a happy child.

A sob broke from her, and the hands on her shoulders
tightened. 'I make you this solemn pledge,' Alex vowed
fiercely. 'No one—will ever—take that laughter away from
her again!'

Tears slid into Mia's eyes. Alex watched them come,
watched her soft mouth begin to quiver, and something
painful seemed to rip free inside him. He shuddered. 'You
are so damned vulnerable sometimes it makes my heart
ache just to look at you!'

So was he, she realised with a shock that stopped her
heart beating altogether. Alex was painfully vulnerable to
her vulnerability!

'Oh!' she choked—why, she didn't even know—but in
the next moment her arms were sliding up and around his

neck, and just as she had done once before without any warning, she buried her face in his throat and clung to him as if her very life depended on it.

How they got from there to kissing feverishly she didn't know either. Or how they ended up in a heated tangle of naked limbs on the bed. But she knew by the time she took him into her body that something very radical had changed in their relationship because there were no barriers, no resenting the way he made her lose control of herself.

'I adore you,' he murmured against her clinging mouth. 'You crept into my heart, without my even knowing how you did it. Now I cannot seem to take a breath without being made aware that you are there, right inside me.'

'I know,' she whispered in soft understanding because he had done the very same thing to her. 'I love you so much that it actually hurts me to think about it.'

He reacted like a man who had been shot in the chest. He stopped moving, stopped breathing. 'Say that again,' he commanded hoarsely.

His eyes were black, his skin pale, his beautiful bone structure taut under stress. Mia lifted gentle fingers to cover those taut cheeks and held those black eyes with her own earnest green ones. 'I love you,' she repeated.

He caught the words in his mouth, stole them, tasted them and made her repeat them over and over again until the whole thing carried them off into one of those wildly hot passionate interludes that had always managed to completely overpower them even when they'd thought they hated each other.

'This is it,' Alex murmured lazily when they were lying, limp-limbed and sated, in each other's arms. 'I will never let you go now.'

'Do you see me trying to get away?' She smiled.

'No.' He frowned. 'But—' A knock sounded at the closed bedroom door.

'Alex!' his brother's voice called out. 'Frazier is on the phone! You had better get down here!'

'Well?' Mia asked anxiously. She was hovering in the doorway of Alex's study where he stood, leaning against the desk behind him, his dark face lost in brooding thought.

He was dressed in the same clothes she had taken off him earlier, whereas she had delayed long enough to drag on a lightweight dress of cool blue cotton, before hurrying downstairs.

He glanced up and smiled, but it was a brief smile. 'He is on his way,' he told her. 'In flight as we speak.'

Mia shivered. 'W-when will he get here?'

'Tomorrow at the earliest.' he replied, then grimaced. 'The airport here does not accept incoming traffic after dark so he has no choice but to stop over in Thessalonika...'

'W-what if he brings the police with him?'

'He is not going to do that.' He sounded so absolutely certain about it that she was almost reassured.

Except that she knew her father. 'Alex...'

'No,' he cut in, and began to walk towards her, his lean face grimly set. 'You are not to worry about this,' he commanded. 'I know what I am doing.'

In other words, he was asking her to trust him.

But it was no longer Alex she didn't trust—it was her father. 'I'm going to find Suzanna,' she murmured, turning away.

He let her go—which only increased her anxiety. It took real effort to lift her mood to meet Suzanna's bubbling effervescence as they explored together this wonderful paradise Suzanna was now calling home.

'You've got to believe in him,' Carol said quietly when she caught Mia in a moment's white-faced introspection while Suzanna was enjoying her bath, before going to bed in the room she had picked out for herself. 'Alex is amazingly efficient when he sets his mind on something.'

'He lost his island.' Mia smiled bleakly at that.

'Ah, but that was because it came down to a straight choice between his old dream and his new one,' Carol explained. 'The new dream won, hand over fist. If it hadn't he wouldn't have given the island up, I can assure you,' she said. 'He has astonishing patience, you see. He would simply have kept you barefoot and pregnant until you produced the son he needed to stake his claim on the island.'

Suzanna interrupted them at that moment, dancing out of the bathroom wrapped in a towel and looking so blissfully happy that Mia firmly thrust her worries away so she could pretend that everything was as wonderful as the child seemed to think it was.

The call that Jack Frazier was on his way from Skiathos airport came very early the next morning while they were all sitting around the breakfast table, trying to look perfectly relaxed.

But, really, the waiting had got to everyone by then. No one ate, except Suzanna. No one spoke much, except Suzanna. In fact, it was all so very fraught that when Alex took the call on his mobile it was almost a relief to know the waiting would soon be over.

'Right,' he said briskly. 'This is it.' He sounded so invigorated that Mia suddenly wanted to hit him! 'Carol, you were going to show Mia and Suzanna your upstairs studio, I believe,' he prompted very smoothly.

'Oh! Yes!' Like a puppet pulled by its master's string, Carol jumped to her feet and turned towards Suzanna. 'Come on, poppet,' she said over-brightly. 'This is going to be fun! Wait until you see the size of the piece of paper we are going to paint a picture on!'

Eager to fall in with any plans, Suzanna scrambled down from her chair and was at Carol's side in a second.

'Mia?' the other woman prompted.

'I'll be there in a minute,' she said, turning anxiously

towards Alex as the other two walked away. 'Tell me what you are going to do!' she pleaded.

'Later,' he promised. 'For now I want you out of sight until your father has been and gone.'

'But—!'

It was as far as she got. 'No!' he exploded, turning angrily on her. 'I will not have you exposed in any way to that man!' he swore. 'So do as you are told, Mia, or, so help me, I will make you do it!'

Her chin came up, her green eyes coming alight with a defiance that showed the old Mia, whom he had spent the whole previous night loving into oblivion, had come rising up out of the ashes of all that time and effort. 'Back to purdah again, I take it!' she said cuttingly.

'He's at the gates.' Leon's voice came shiveringly flat-toned from just behind her.

'Damn and blast it, woman!' Alex rasped out frustrat-edly, and in the next moment Mia found herself cradled high in his arms and he was striding up the stairs with a face apparently carved from granite.

He dumped her on a chair in her bedroom. 'Stay!' he commanded. Then he strode angrily back out of the room, slamming the door shut behind him.

She stayed. She stayed exactly where she was as she listened to the sound of a car coming down the driveway, listened to it stop outside the house, heard a door slam— shuddered and closed her eyes on a wave of nausea when she heard her father's voice bark something very angry. She heard Leon's dark-toned level reply, heard footsteps sound-ing on the veranda floor...

Then nothing. The whole villa seemed to settle into an ominous silence. She tolerated it for a while, just sat there and let that silence wash over her for several long wretched, muscle-locking minutes.

But that was the limit of her endurance, and the next

moment she was up, stiff-limbed and shaking, walking out of the bedroom and to the head of the polished stairway.

As she moved downwards she could see the study door standing half-open, and hear the rasp of her father's voice as he blasted words at Alex.

As if drawn by something way beyond instinct, she walked silently towards that half-open doorway.

'I don't know what you think you're damned well playing at!' She heard her father's angry voice as she approached. 'But you won't get away with it!'

'Get away with what?' was Alex's bland reply.

'You know what I'm talking about!' Jack Frazier grated.

Mia saw him then, and went perfectly still. He was standing with his back to her, every inch of him pulsing with a blistering fury as he faced Alex across the width of the desk. Alex was seated, looking supremely at ease in the way he was lazing back in his chair, his dark eyes cool, his lean face arrogantly impassive.

But what really struck at the very heart of her was to see Leon, standing at his brother's shoulder.

Her breath stilled, her eyes widening as she instantly realised just what she was looking at. It was like being shot back to another scene like this—in another study, in another country altogether. Only here the roles had been reversed. This time it was her father who was pulsing with anger and frustration and Alex who was looking utterly unmoved by it all.

Leon's sole purpose was to stand silent witness, whereas in London it had been Mia who had played that role.

A deliberate set-up? she wondered, and suspected that it most probably was. Jack Frazier had humiliated Alex that day when he had made him surrender his pride in front of Mia. Now it was her father's turn to know just what that felt like.

She shivered, not sure that she liked to see Alex displaying this depth of ruthlessness.

'All I know,' she heard Alex reply, 'is that you have been standing here, throwing out a lot of threats and insults, but I am still no wiser as to exactly what it is you are actually angry about.'

'Don't play bloody games with me,' her father grated. 'You've reneged on our deal, you cheating bastard! And you've stolen my youngest daughter! I want her back right now—or I'll have you arrested for abduction!'

'The telephone sits right there. By all means,' Alex said invitingly, 'call the police if you feel this passionate about it. But I think I should warn you,' he added silkily, 'that the police will demand proof of your claim before they will act. You have brought that proof with you, I must presume?'

Silence. It suddenly consumed the very atmosphere. Mia's spine began to tingle, her breath lying suspended in her chest while her eyes fixed themselves on her father's back as she waited for him to produce the proof that she of all people knew he had.

Yet...he didn't do anything! He just stood there, unmoving, in that steadily thickening silence.

It was Alex who broke it. 'You have a problem with that?' he questioned smoothly.

'We don't need to get the police involved in this if you are sensible!' her father said irritably.

'Sensible,' Alex thoughtfully repeated. 'Yes,' he said agreeably, 'I think I can be *sensible* about this. You show *me* your proof of claim, and I will hand Suzanna over to you with no more argument.'

Mia felt the blood freeze in her veins, an excruciating sense of pained betrayal whitening her face as she took a jerky step forward. Then her pained eyes suddenly clashed head-on with a pair of burning black ones as Alex finally saw her there, and she went perfectly still.

No! those eyes seemed to be telling her. Wait! Trust me!

Trust him. Her hand reached out to clutch at the polished

doorframe. Trust him! her mind was screaming at her. If you don't, you will lose him! He will never forgive you!

Trust him. She swallowed thickly over the lump of fear that had formed in her throat and remained where she was.

'I keep that kind of stuff with my lawyers,' her father snapped out impatiently, 'not on my person!'

Mia lost Alex's attention as he fixed it back on Jack Frazier. 'I possess all the usual communication equipment,' he pointed out. 'Call up your lawyers, tell them to fax the relevant information here and all this unpleasantness could be over in minutes.'

He even rose to lift the telephone receiver off its hook and held it out to her father! His body was relaxed, his face utterly impassive, and he did not so much as flicker another glance in Mia's direction as a new silence began to stretch endlessly, along with Mia's nerve-ends as she stood there, clutching the wooden doorframe with fingers that had turned to ice.

Then she jumped, startled as Alex suddenly slammed the telephone back on its rest. 'No,' he said through gritted teeth. 'You cannot do it, can you, because there was no official adoption!'

His hand shot out, picking up something from the desk and then slapping it back down again in front of Jack Frazier.

'You conned Mia into believing she was signing away all rights to her baby,' he bit out, 'when in reality what she did sign was not worth the damned paper it was written on!'

Her father was staring down at whatever it was that Alex had slapped down in front of him. Mia's eyelashes fluttered as she, too, looked down at the desk where she could just see a corner of a sickeningly familiar document.

It was her own copy of what her father had made her sign seven years ago. It had to be. Alex must have gone through her private papers, without her knowing it.

'She did sign it, though!' Jack Frazier suddenly hit back jeeringly. 'In fact, she was only too bloody eager to hand over her bastard child to me!'

'Oh,' Mia gasped, having to push an icy fist up against her mouth to stop the sound from escaping.

He wasn't even bothering to deny it!

'Or be out on the streets, as you so charitably put it at the time!' Alex tagged on scathingly. 'You played on her youth, her naïvety, her desperation and her inability to tell a legal document from absolute garbage!' he went on. 'And you did it all with a cold-blooded heartless cruelty that must make her very happy that you are *not* her real father!'

'What's that supposed to mean?' Jack Frazier jerked out.

'This is what it means...' Another piece of paper landed on the desk. 'Your blood group,' he said curtly, then slapped another piece of paper on top of it. 'Karl Dansing's blood group.' Another piece of paper arrived the same way. 'And finally—thankfully—my wife's blood group!' Alex said with grim satisfaction. 'Note the odd one out?' he prompted bitingly.

'Any questions?' he then asked. 'No, I thought not, because you knew this already, didn't you? Which is why you have been punishing her all these bloody years. Well...' He leaned forward, his dark face a map of blistering contempt for the other man. 'It is now over,' he said. 'And you are no longer welcome here.'

'But what's the matter with you, man?' Jack Frazier blustered in angry frustration. Something had gone wrong with all his careful planning and he still had not worked out exactly what that something was. 'If I am prepared to accept Mia as my daughter, then the damned island is yours when she gives birth to my grandson!'

'But Mia is not carrying your grandson,' Alex coolly contradicted. 'She is carrying my daughter.'

'What? You mean she couldn't even get that right?'

Dark eyes suddenly began to look very dangerous.

'Watch what you say here,' Alex warned. 'This is my home—and my wife—you are maligning.'

'A wife you didn't damned well want in the first place!' Jack Frazier said scornfully. 'But if you've decided to keep her, there will be other children no doubt—sons!' he added covetously. 'All you have to do is give me back Suzanna, and Mia will be as compliant as a pussy cat, I promise you. Another year and you could still have your island!'

'You can keep the island,' Alex countered coldly. 'I have no wish to set foot on it again. In fact,' he added, 'you have nothing I want that I have not already taken away from you. Which makes you defunct as far as any of my family are concerned. So, as you once put it so eloquently to me—the door, Mr Frazier, is over there.'

'But—!'

'Get him out of here,' Alex grated at his brother, his face drawn into taut lines of utter disgust.

Leon moved, and so did Mia, jolting out of the stasis that had been holding her to move shakily back to the stairs. She had no wish to come face to face with Jack Frazier. She had no wish to set eyes on him ever again.

She was standing by the bedroom window when Alex came looking for her.

'I hope you are pleased with yourself,' he said in a clipped voice.

'Not really.' She turned to send him a wryly apologetic smile. He still looked angry, his beautiful olive skin paler than it should have been. 'I almost blew that for you,' she admitted. 'I'm sorry.'

'Why did you come down there when I specifically asked you not to?'

'I don't know.' She shrugged. 'It was a—compulsion. I couldn't see any way that you could make him give up Suzanna, without giving him what he wanted, you see.'

'And in return for your lack of trust in me you learned

a whole lot more about yourself than you actually wanted to know!'

That made her eyes flash. 'I learned that you had the bare-faced cheek to go through my private papers!' she hit back indignantly.

'Ah...' At least he had the grace to grimace guiltily at that one. The anger died out of him, his warm hands sliding around her body to draw her close. 'I was desperately in love with a woman who refused to trust me as far as she could throw me,' he murmured in his own defence. 'Men that desperate do desperate things. Forgive me?' he pleaded, bending his dark head so he could nuzzle her ear.

Mia wasn't ready to forgive anyone anything. Her head moved back, away from that diverting mouth. 'When did you go through my private papers?' she demanded to know.

He sighed, his smile at her stubbornness rueful. 'I came straight here after leaving you in London,' he told her. 'Initially, I wanted to see if there was any way we could reverse the adoption,' he explained, 'but the moment I read that damned thing I knew it was not legal!' His angry sigh brushed her face.

'But I needed to get that confirmed with my own lawyers before I dared take action. And you had signed it, *agape mou*,' he added gently. 'My lawyers were afraid that if I faced your father with what I had discovered while you were still in London, he could have used the fact you had signed away your right to Suzanna to make the child a ward of the British courts while we fought over her.'

'And thereby gain himself a different way of blackmailing us into doing what he wanted us to do.' Mia nodded understandingly.

'It was safer for me to get you both here to Greece before I faced him with what I knew.'

'So you kidnapped us.'

'Yes.' He sighed. 'I'm sorry if I frightened you.'

Frightened her? He'd put her through a hell of uncer-

tainty over the last twenty-four hours! 'You are as under-
hand and cunning as my father,' she said accusingly. 'Do
you know that?'

'I love you madly,' he murmured coaxingly. 'I would
not hurt a hair on your beautiful head.'

In answer to that blatant bit of seduction, Mia turned her
back on him again—though she made no attempt to move
out of those strong arms still holding her.

And Alex was not going to stop the verbal seduction. 'I
adore you,' he whispered softly against her ear. 'I *ache* for
you night and day I am so badly bitten.'

'Which is why you keep a mistress, I suppose.'

As a mood-killer it worked like a dream. His dark head
lifted. 'Ah,' he said ruefully once more. 'The mistress. You
are after your pound of flesh again, I think.'

I want more than a pound of your flesh, Alexander
Doumas, Mia thought covetously. I want it all! 'I apologise,' she said with deceptive contrition. 'I forgot for the
moment that I am contracted not to mention the mistress.'

He laughed, not fooled at all by her tone, and the arms
holding her tightened their grip. 'There is no mistress,' he
informed her drily. 'And there never *was* a mistress.' His
mouth was tasting her ear again. 'I have not looked at another woman since the first night I saw you across a
crowded room and was instantly smitten—as I suspect you
already know!'

Mia smiled a smile of feline satisfaction. 'Carol did imply something of the kind,' she confessed, and arched her
neck to give him greater access to the ear lobe he was
tasting. 'I just wanted to hear you say it.'

'I'm going to rip that crazy contract up...' he promised.

'Good,' she said approvingly.

'And make you sign another one that will tie you to me
for life,' he added.

'What makes you think I will sign it?' she challenged.

His mouth moved to her throat, his tongue arrowing directly for a particular pulse point he knew all about. 'I have my ways,' he murmured against that exact spot—and laughed softly as she drew in a sharp, shaken gasp of air. Her body was already beginning to throb in his arms with pleasure when a sound outside caught her attention.

Glancing downwards, she saw Suzanna appear, with Carol and Leon in tow. They were dressed for swimming, with towels draped around their necks. Hand in hand, they walked off towards the swimming pool area.

'She has them wrapped around her little finger,' Mia drily remarked.

'I know the feeling,' Alex murmured. 'Her mama has me tied up the same way.'

Mia smiled and said nothing, her gaze following the trio until they disappeared out of sight, then she lifted her gaze to the larger view of this, her new home. Out beyond the gardens the sea was shimmering lazily, and beyond it stood the misted green-grey string of smaller islands.

'Which is your island?' she asked.

He didn't answer for a long moment, seemingly much more interested in tasting her. Then his dark head came up. 'The one you can see directly in front of us,' he said, 'with the two crescent-shaped patches of golden beach...'

Is that why he had bought this villa, she wondered, because it looked out on his true home?

'Your vision,' she sighed. 'I'm so sorry you lost it.'

'I'm not,' he replied, with no hint of regret. 'Visions can change. Mine has changed. All I want is right here with me, in my arms.'

'Still,' Mia said sadly, 'it seems so very unfair that you have to break a promise to your father because my so-called father is such a dreadful man.'

'I have you,' he said. 'I have my child, growing inside you.' His hands splayed across her abdomen in a gesture of warm possession. 'And I have a miniature version of you in Suzanna, who worships the very ground I walk upon because I rescued her from your father. I am very content, believe me.'

'Well, your contentment is going to fly right out of this window if you move your hands much lower,' she informed him quite pragmatically—then tilted her head, her green eyes twinkling wickedly up at him.

And he laughed, a deep, dark, very masculine sound that had her turning in his arms to face him. That was all it took. Their bodies fused...so did their mouths...and they were lost in each other.

If you enjoyed what you just read,
then we've got an offer you can't resist!

Take 2 bestselling love stories FREE!
Plus get a FREE surprise gift!

Coming Next Month

#2037 THE SPANISH GROOM Lynne Graham
To please his ailing godfather, Cesar Valverde agreed to marry Dixie Robinson. Unexpectedly, he found her to be an achingly sensual woman. So within a week, his fake fiancée had become his wife and become pregnant!

#2038 THE SECRET MISTRESS Emma Darcy
Presents Passion
Luis Martinez had never forgiven Shontelle for walking away from their affair. But now she needed his help, and Luis saw a way to exact vengeance for his wounded pride: he'd keep her safe in exchange for one night in her bed...

#2039 TO WOO A WIFE Carole Mortimer
Bachelor Brothers
As a beautiful, young widow, Abbie was wary of emotional and physical involvement. Jarrett was used to being a winner in the boardroom and the bedroom, so to him, Abbie was the ultimate challenge: she needed wooing!

#2040 HE'S MY HUSBAND! Lindsay Armstrong
Nicola was Brett's wife of convenience, but it seemed to her that he had other admirers. Nicola loved Brett and his children, so the time had come to show everyone, including Brett, exactly whose husband he really was!

#2041 THE UNEXPECTED BABY Diana Hamilton
Expecting!
Elena was deeply in love with her brand-new husband, Jed, so discovering she was pregnant should have completed her joy. Elena knew she'd have to tell Jed, but would their marriage survive the truth?

#2042 REMARRIED IN HASTE Sandra Field
Brant Curtis had dreamed about his ex-wife, Rowan, for years, and now he was face-to-face with her. He didn't have a plan, but he wanted more than a one night stand for old times' sake—he wanted his wife back, whatever it took!

In July 1999 Harlequin Superromance®
brings you *The Lyon Legacy*—a
brand-new 3-in-1 book from popular
authors Peg Sutherland, Roz Denny Fox
& Ruth Jean Dale

3 stories for the price of 1!

Join us as we celebrate
Harlequin's 50th Anniversary!

Look for these other
Harlequin Superromance®
titles wherever books are sold July 1999:

A COP'S GOOD NAME (#846)
by Linda Markowiak

THE MAN FROM HIGH MOUNTAIN (#848)
by Kay David

HER OWN RANGER (#849)
by Anne Marie Duquette

SAFE HAVEN (#850)
by Evelyn A. Crowe

JESSIE'S FATHER (#851)
by C. J. Carmichael